Comments on works by I. Michael Grossman

"Reading *Shrinkwrapped*, it felt very much like the author left his ego at the door and gave it to the reader straight on. I'll gloss over the fact that the writing was crystal-clear, composed with an economy of just-right words and phrases that stopped me for moments to reflect and enjoy and then left me wondering anxiously how the trajectory of his life would turn out. The lessons worked on and learned are lessons we all have to learn, in one fashion or another. The author shows us that we are all flawed, have led imperfect lives, and that it's okay, but that in order to find peace and love, there is work to be done.

"Presenting us with his "journey", in what seems total recall, places us comfortably and uncomfortably in his head and we root for his enlightenment as we hope for our own and sigh happily that in the end or perhaps in the "now" you have made it through.

"Grossman has written and will continue to write many fine books of poetry and stories...but I suspect that this is his magnum opus...the book that needed to be written and is written brilliantly. Bravo!"

Yvette Nachmias-Baeu, author of *A Reluctant Life,*
Clara at Sixty, Best Friends, and *Ledicia's Key*

———

"...widely praised for its insights of psychotherapy."
Michigan State University Book Review Newsletter

THE ACCIDENTAL PRESIDENT

An Intergalactic Guide to Homo Sapiens

I. Michael Grossman

Publisher's Information

Author contact: imichaelgrossman@gmail.com
Website and blog: ebookbakery.com

ISBN 978-1-953080-29-5
Library of Congress Control Number: 2022915052

EBookBakery

TABLE OF CONTENTS

ACKNOWLEDGMENTS

Thank you, thank you, thank you:
Bill Azano
Nancy Azano
Hal Crook
Ken Dautrick
Lauren Davenport (the superior writer)
Enid Flaherty
Dr. Gene McKee
Tracy Hart
Gene Kincaid
Camilla Lee
Susan Mandel
Jane McCarthy
Yvette Nachmais-Baeu
Dr. Robert Reece
Theresa Schimmel
Bill Seymour
Peter Stonberg
James Transue

And for moral and caloric support:
Dot Distal
Susan Blume
Debbie Bowley
Lenore Maroney
Jay Montecalvo
Lisa Montecalvo

DEDICATION

Susan and Lauren

Asked about humanity's place in the cosmos,
Carl Sagan's assessment was that:

*"We live on an insignificant planet
of a humdrum star,
lost in a galaxy,
tucked away in some forgotten
corner of a universe."*

———————

By contrast, astrophysicist Howard Smith suggests
we're a miraculous accident:

*Until we know more, we must acknowledge
that the evolution of intelligent life could be the result
of an astronomically unlikely sequence of events.*

Howard A. Smith, Joanna Neborsky

1

Before

The fields flooded again, and with his wheat crop threatened, Jeremiah Butler wasn't watching the lottery on TV that night. 269 million sets were tuned to the drawing which Neilson reported was the largest audience ever. Viewership dwarfed even 2017 when Powerball winner Mavis L. Wanczyk scored a check for $758,700,000.

Despite record-breaking viewership, this winning lottery ticket paid nothing. Yet CNB simulcast the show in all four-hundred thirty languages actively spoken in America – from Angloromani (a creole English language spoken by Romani Americans) to Yiddish.

Every native-born American who had resided in the USA for at least fourteen years and was thirty-five or older, was automatically entered. Lottery organizers, the Selons, chose those qualifications for a reason. They wanted to echo the requirements set in the American Constitution for Presidential eligibility, thinking it gave the lottery the feel of legitimacy. There would be only one winner, and like the lottery during the war in Vietnam, if your number was drawn, you were drafted. Service wasn't voluntary.

In days preceding the drawing, Americans, never hesitant with opinions, were permitted to voice disapproval. The Selons allowed protests and citizens marched in scores of U.S. cities, assembling with megaphones and magic-marker placards. Crowds shouted insults knowing they wouldn't accomplish much. But at least they'd rallied against Selon authority.

President Bernard Gammon, the 55th American President, continued to deliver impassioned speeches against the lottery until he fell to the plague, and illness forever silenced his booming Texas twang. His Vice

President, Eleanor Winslow, was prepared to assume the highest office, but the Selons made clear they would not allow her succession.

Before the plague took him – in the time of the Great Fires and Floods – President Gammon tried to comfort Americans. In his State of the Union address, he promised that the havoc reaped by weather extremes – tornado force winds that came without meteorological warning to rip homes off foundations – weeks of crop-withering heat and the floods – that these were cyclical events. Skies would cool, Gammon promised, fields would dry, and the crisis would abate.

Gammon's Cabinet secretaries echoed his message in copycat speeches, reminding constituents that Earth had been around for 4.5 billion years and would continue to rotate on axis long after these momentary challenges passed. Off the record though, several worried that humanity could face extinction – and a few were so politically brash as to suggest human mismanagement was a factor.

But the chaos did not abate, and tidal floods spilled oceans over the land, polluting aquifers until drinkable water became scarce. Even the stored harvests of the great corporate farms proved inadequate, and as they depleted, armies marched to corner dwindling food supplies. Earth divided into clusters of the well-fed and the emaciated have-nots.

Around the time that President Gammon passed, the Selon Parliament met to decide if it was time to reveal their presence.

2

THE TEST

IN THE STARLIT Chamber of Decision, thirteen billion light-years from Earth, Eminence called Parliament to order. "Seer will summarize the state of Milky Way Galaxy planets and his recommendations before we vote."

"Your Eminence, fellow Selons," Seer began, "as we have for eons, our teams visited the hundred billion planets we supervise. Several hundred required remediation. I'm pleased to report only three are red flagged. They are:

"Draugr (or PSR B1257+12A) for its rapid deterioration due to low mass - somewhat half that of earth's moon. A density-infusion squad was dispatched.

"KELT-9b, one of the Milky Way's hottest planets with a surface reaching 4,600 Kelvin. We've seeded it with a hundred billion tons of Graupel to lower its temperature.

"Which leaves Earth, a planet facing existential threats," said Seer, "and though we propose superficial abatements, they address symptoms, not the root of Earth's fragility. The threats facing Earth are such that without more aggressive intervention, we'll have to deal with the planet endlessly. The core of the difficulties is Earth's greatest irritant – a uniquely irrational species – the homo sapiens. We've long been entertained by them - amused by their unwillingness to address existential issues despite a scientific community that offers the rational solutions humans routinely ignore. Besides their limited ability to reason, we find evidence of a moral deficiency, possibly genetic. Selon intervention is unavoidable, but it begs the question: how aggressive should we be?"

The attending Selons radiated agreement. Seer was much admired for a shrewd assessment of peculiar species.

"I have a question, Seer." said Provost Darius glowing with interest.

"Of course, Provost Darius," said Seer.

"Why consider intervention when it violates the Prime Directive? Aren't we compelled to let humans plod along to their own extinction?"

"And what's more," Commander Gregor interrupted Darius before Seer could answer, "I don't recall any galactic importance to homo sapiens. There are merely 8 billion of them, and their sun flames out in a billion years."

"Correct on both accounts, Darius and Gregor," said Seer, "and normally we'd let them self-destruct. But Earth has Xonium."

"I was unaware," said Provost Darius.

"And of course the Second Directive instructs us to protect Xonium anywhere we find it, given its importance for intergalactic travel. Earth's coastlines are loaded with it, and thankfully humans doesn't know it," said Seer.

"But isn't Proxima Centauri richer with Xonium?" said Darius. "Why bother with Earth given it's a planet in chaos?"

"Proxima Centauri's deposits are substantial, Darius. But the Treaty? The Aarebets hold mining rights ..."

"... Ah, the Aarebet Treaty. I'd forgotten," said Darius.

"So Earth matters," said Seer.

"But tell me," Provost Darius continued, "since our present Xonium supply is adequate for a billion years, why violate the Prime Directive now?"

"It has to do with human negligence," said Seer. "Earth's depleted ozone layer causes the rising waters to alter its geography. Twenty-nine percent of the planet's surface is land mass, and while the planet has actually gained land surface in the last thirty years - an amount about the size of its Lake Michigan - erosion along the planet's coastlines threatens the Xonium."

"Then obviously we have to intervene," said Commander Gregor who enjoyed celebrity among the Selons for his skill eradicating useless species.

"My team has an opening and can do away with them immediately. Shall I handle it in the usual manner, Eminence?"

"A moment now, Gregor," Provost Darius interrupted. "There must be there less destructive ways to handle them?"

"Always so timid, Provost Darius," said Commander Gregor flashing annoyance. "Will the time ever come when you appreciate efficiency? My teams can dissolve the species like that - Gregor fired a bolt of light across the chamber. Recall the Doridians. After my recent visit, they bother us no more."

"We admire your professionalism, Commander Gregor" said Eminence who's powerful presence caused the chamber to still and attendees to give the meeting leader their rapt attention. "But the Council of Overseers asks if eliminating the homo sapiens is the preferred solution. We know the Council is all about the Prime Directive. They believe humans have evidenced merit on occasion and ask us to explore their nature."

"A total waste of time, with respect Eminence," said Commander Gregor. "Given the history of the human species, could Parliament possibly expect altruism from those creatures? They're a stone's throw away from walking on all fours. Don't we have issues of consequence to address?"

"You may eradicate if our analysis concludes homo sapiens are beyond hope," said Eminence.

"Not *if* but *when*," said Commander Gregor.

"I disagree and applaud that Parliament proceeds carefully," said Provost Darius. "The loss of even an insignificant species diminishes the richness of the entire Galaxy. And I'm of the opinion that the human problem isn't species systemic but stems from how hopelessly they govern. Help them revamp its mechanisms, and I'm sure you'll see they can prioritize planet and tribe over personal greed."

"Perhaps," said Eminence, "but that is the question, and Seer will direct our analysis of them. He has identified a tribe to examine. His Petrie dish of choice is the dominant Americans since their constitution directs them to value every citizen."

"They are my subjects of choice," said Seer. "I picked a democracy and not an autocracy or oligarchy since the latter unabashedly exist to benefit their elite," said Seer. "Nor will I test a government where the leaders came to power by birthright. Neither autocrats nor royals would provide what Earth needs."

"If you think you'll find altruism among American legislators, I'd like some of the Neptunian dust you've absorbed," said Commander Gregor.

"I didn't say I was optimistic, Gregor," said Seer, "but the Overseers ask us to test."

"To determine what exactly?" said Darius.

"Does the tribe have the capacity to govern? The answer is predetermined if we let them pick leaders through their present flawed electoral mechanisms. To allow that would be, in the words of an Earth mathematician with Selon-like intelligence, 'the definition of insanity'."

"Seer found intelligence?" said Gregor.

"It exists," said Seer. "But it can't impact how they act unless we shake up how they govern," said Seer. "The first American President understood the need to revamp government. When asked to start a line of royalty. Washington refused, preferring elections. But despite his inspired instinct, it took only a few terms for the flaws in their electoral process to became blatant.

"What's wrong with how they pick leaders?" said Darius.

"Seriously, Darius. Sometimes you obtuseness astounds me," said Gregor.

"Show restraint, Gregor," said Eminence.

"Inherent in their elections," said Seer, "is a certainty that in time it favors men driven to acquire power. An unintended consequence is that more and more energy is spent to rest wealth and authority from its citizens. Before an Earth century passed, the first president's hopes for a democracy drifted into oligarchy - though the leaders still branded it a democracy. The tribe is easy to indoctrinate."

"You make my point," said Gregor. "Flawed species, flawed government."

"Perhaps not, Gregor. Their mechanisms to govern are clearly flawed, but that doesn't prove humans couldn't be altruistic if they had systems that function," said Seer. "That's what we want to find out."

"So Seer's test will…?"

"… determine if fresh leadership can release any potential in humans to act for the good of all members," said Seer. "If it's determined that self-interest will always drive them, Commander Gregor may unleash his team."

"I don't approve of '*unleash*'," said Gregor.

"Let's not rush to judgment," said Provost Darius. "Gregor ignores pages of examples of human compassion in Seer's report. Healthcare workers who risk infection; volunteers who wade floods to carry food to the homeless; many who care for their planet's lesser creatures. Are we to ignore entire sections covering human generosity?"

"Really Darius? You think human history is a meteor shower of joy and kindness. It's war and pestilence." said Gregor.

"The species is 'a bag of mix' if I have it the human expression right," said Eminence. "For example, you have church crusades that brought men to war, but also parishioners generously sharing what they have."

"Commander Gregor doesn't talk about their goodness because his lust to destroy warps his ability to see their nature," said Darius.

"We're wasting time," said Gregor. "Galactically speaking, humans are primitives. They still believe the galaxy originates from some God with a magic wand. They're devout science deniers. How many centuries did it take for a couple of Greeks to argue the Earth isn't flat? How many more centuries passed before they stopped jailing any who subscribed to sphericity? Homo sapiens aren't the galaxies' most sophisticated organisms."

"Yet Seer found intelligence," said Darius. "… that mathematician Seer quoted."

"I'll give you this," said Gregor. "Humans have a sense of humor. As proof I offer the joke they tell about how their God created the world in six Earth-days and rested on the seventh. Upon observing his creation Man, God noted, 'Perhaps I overestimated my ability.'"

"No!" voiced one of the assembled. "Don't tell me Earthlings still anthropomorphize deities?"

"They do," said Gregor.

"They still talk of God in human form?" said another.

"There's a telling passage in one of their holy books, the Talmud - Sanhedrin 38b - authored by one of the oldest of human tribes, the Israelites," said Gregor. "It tells of the creation of Man. When the Holy One, their God, decides to create the species, he materialized a group of angels to help him. Angels are an Earthling metaphor denoting ethereal, superior creatures – like us except they aren't real. Anyway, God asks his angels what they think of his plan to make man in his own image. The angels advise not to create man at all. So God destroys those angels, creates a second group, and asks them the same question. Again, the angels warn against creating man. God destroys the second group of angels. God creates a third group and once again asks the question. The angels answer that God is only going to ignore their advice, and, as master of the universe, he should do as he wishes. So, God creates man. In no time at all it became obvious that his creature is hopelessly flawed. So God sends a great flood to destroy all men. My point," said Gregor, "is that even Talmudic scholars knew man is flawed. I say, finish them off."

"That's not authorized yet, Gregor," said Eminence. "We will test first, and I favor Seer's plan to give them a new head of government - one not doomed by their flawed electoral process ... a president picked at random."

"At random? Isn't it wiser to search among them for one with high intelligence and demonstrated altruism?" said Darius.

"The point is to explore the essential nature of the species," said Eminence, "not to find some rare talent. Seer will circumvent their system of elections to give them a leader unencumbered by allegiance to entrenched power. Their present electoral system can never accomplish that. The third American president warned of the danger of not refreshing the mechanics of government since the mechanisms degrade. He called for a regular dismantling of their institutions even if accomplished violently:

> *The tree of liberty must be refreshed from time to time*
> *with the blood of patriots & tyrants.*
> *It is its natural manure.'"*

"He had the right idea, but hopefully we won't have to spill blood," said Darius.

"A waste of time," said Gregor. "Give them new leadership and they'll repeat human history. Restart the clock a dozen times, but the ill-informed will choose leaders based on charisma and quickly recreate their world of haves and have-nots. Wealth will aggregate as it always has."

"We're about to find that out," said Seer.

"And when your test fails," said Gregor, "get in touch."

"If the new leader fails, we'll have respected the Prime Directive, and you'll get to annihilate, Gregor. With man gone, Earth will stabilize quickly. It's violent climate will calm, the oceans will recede, and the Xonium will be safe," said Eminence.

"Parliament moves like an earth snail," said Gregor.

"One more question," said Darius. "What makes us think the Americans will accept a leader who comes to office without the perceived legitimacy of an election? They'd view it as a *coup d'etat?* And if inaugurated, how would that leader stay in office without the support of the military and the financial backing of those who buy Presidents?"

"When we make ourselves known to Earthlings, it will be in a manner that leaves no doubt. Any who interfere will experience the less gentle side of Selonian nature."

"Well, the plan is unique," said another attendee. "But how will the selection be random?"

"It's all set. Among the lengthy list of human vices, they love to gamble. They're bettors by nature, a card playing, roll-of-the-dice lot, especially fond of a game of chance they call a 'lottery'. Humans love the lottery because it appeals to their instinct to ignore math. A lottery is a random selection against improbable odds, motivated by unlikely reward. But human greed and a proclivity to fantasize make it easy for them to dismiss the laws of probability. Human irrationality makes a lottery the perfect vehicle for leadership selection."

"So, Earth's dominant tribe, the Americans, will get their 56th President from a lottery."

"Then the test result is determined," said Gregor beaming.

"Don't be so sure," said Darius.

3

Disappearing Act

FAMILIES GATHERED AROUND TVs the night of the drawing; others leaned into the bar at their favorite watering hole; students streamed on cellphones, all waiting to learn the name of the next President of the United State of America.

Some imagined an unlikely future for themselves despite the odds. "I have as good a chance as any," said a few. Those inclined to see auras were certain their name would be drawn. Having considered the burdens of office, the more thoughtful prayed their name wouldn't be drawn.

The Selons had made their presence known months before the drawing by dramatically interrupting television shows across the globe. Screens flickered, then turned dark until a Selon avatar appeared, a mask-like alien interpretation of a face in ornate pewter silver. It wavered silently, ghost-like on screens everywhere from televisions to tablets to smart phones. The interruption created havoc. Executives with commercials scheduled to air screamed for their lawyer. Viewers engrossed in their favorite soaps flooded the networks with calls and emails flaming station managers. What could be so important that they would interrupt *The Real Housewives?*

The Selon avatar flickered silently. Older, experienced viewers told puzzled younger ones that this was nothing more than a *War-of-the-Worlds*-fashioned prank. But it was soon apparent that something more unprecedented was happening.

In a computer-generated voice, the avatar began to speak, its mechanical voice warned in stilted syllables that humans had bungled their job as Earth's caretakers. The avatar – its speech quickly becoming more natural - began to detail the failures of the human species – from its refusal to address the planet's depleted ozone layer to civic dysfunctionality, economic disparities, judicial injustice, gun violence and racial and religious cruelties. It listed in chronological order a string of pandemics - deadly viruses linked to man's careless farming of animals. It reviewed the impact of climate change – the droughts, fires and water shortages even as rising seas turned aquifers to brine. Blunder upon blunder, it said, left Earth teetering and homo sapiens near extinction.

The avatar advised that they, the Selons, had for thousands of years been minding the Milky Way Galaxy and, with Earth in dire jeopardy, it was time to address that homo sapiens had ignored their planet's needs. Since Earth's calamities resulted from human mismanagement, the avatar continued, Selons would evaluate the human capacity to govern, focusing initially on Earth's dominant tribe – the Americans. Since new leadership was obviously required, Vice President Eleanor Winslow would not be permitted to succeed the just-deceased President Gammon. A new President would be picked by lottery.

The Selon proclamation that a centuries-old, election-based democracy must accept a president chosen by lottery enraged Americans on both sides of the political aisle. The constitution, written by cherished forefathers admired for their foresight, specified that the president should be designated by the Electoral College. In unprecedented unanimity, congressional leaders joined crowds in the streets with signs and clenched fists - the most strident opposition coming from the corporate elite. They'd spent good money to put presidents in the Oval, and they weren't about take orders from a TV avatar that had never written a check.

Following the Selon announcement, Vice President Eleanor Winslow hastily assembled the press and made clear she would not comply. The American people needed assurance that their government would carry on as constitutionally mandated; that her succession was imperative, and she'd damn well see it happen. She noted that, yes, Earth had a few problems, but Congress had honored the American tradition to ignore them. Records proved that the climate had always been in flux, never mind that high seas had recently swallowed Norfolk. "Don't believe what you see," the Vice President insisted. "The flooding is nothing more than the ebb and flow of ocean levels as they've shifted for centuries."

The Selons responded to VP Winslow with a second television appearance. The avatar gave her forty-eight earth hours to resign … or else. VP Winslow's staff assured her that the Selons couldn't prevent her succession; the threat was a bluff. They explained that the only power the Selons had was the ability to hack the networks – a nifty technological trick - but hardly persuasive.

Congressional leaders rushed to podiums to condemn the Selon hacker and scoff at claims it was interplanetary. "Such fake news is an insult to American intelligence," said Kentucky's Senator Rubin Hallingsworth. "Who's going to believe human intelligence has anything to do with Earth's sorry state? And worse than talk of planetary crisis," continued the Senator, "by hacking the airwaves the Selons interrupted the soaps."

The United Nations Security Council rushed into session to draft a proclamation in support of VP Winslow's succession, applauding her bold refusal to cancel the scheduled inauguration. The fifteen Council ambassadors stood in solidarity to assure that should anything similar threaten their own nation's leader, they wouldn't be swayed by some crudely fashioned digital mannequin. "Hell, Pixar creates better-looking anime than that clown," noted America's Ambassador to the UN.

In a ping-pong debate, the Selon avatar appeared a third time. "Since VP Winslow has not stepped down, Earthlings will be taught to respect a Selon request. An example will be made of Kentucky's Senator Hallingsworth for having urged VP Winslow to stay in office. The senator will showcase Selon authority."

The following night the lights dimmed in Frankfort, Kentucky's seat of government, as Senator Hallingsworth stood at the podium to speak in support of Winslow. His teleprompter scrolled as he urged Americans to pay no attention to the avatar. The Senator was adding self-congratulatory remarks about the new pork-barrel football stadium he brought to Frankfort when the mic went dead in his hand. Viewers saw his lips move but no sound. Aides rushed to tap his mic as wide-eyed viewers saw Senator Hollingsworth start to fade in bunches of pixels until nothing remained but his empty suit in a pile at the podium. Sets darkened, and smartphone screens dissolved and the ghost-like Selon avatar appeared to explain that for his opposition, the Kentucky Senator had been dismantled. As punishment, henceforth Kentucky would be a state with only one senator. With what press later described as a hint of smirk, the avatar gave Eleanor Winslow one last chance to resign by morning or she would experience Hollingsworth's fate. She was to vacate her office and, like a common citizen, await the name of the new President of the United States once the lottery picked a winner.

Inclined not to believe their eyes, Kentucky's six congressional representatives joined hands on the capital steps in Frankfort to voice their opposition. Vice President Winslow announced there were no Selons. She subscribed to the theory offered by the Director of the CIA that the avatar was a gimmick with the Chinese behind the whole thing. The Director himself confirmed Selons weren't real, and said he had indisputable proof that the pixel-by-pixel dissolution of Kentucky's Senator was mere holography. That annoyed the Selons enough to dissolve the Director during his Fox News interview.

Despite the demonstrations of Selon power, a number of senators stood with Eleanor Winslow in support of the China Conspiracy Theory. "Provide proof," they dared the Selons. The Selons accommodated by dissolving leaders in a half-dozen countries, leaving empty chairs in palaces and offices from India to Saudi Arabia.

The power of the Selons began to sink in. Representatives from both houses of Congress who'd stood with Winslow reminded constituents that they'd believed in the Selons all along, insisting that they'd repeatedly urged Winslow to resign, if unbeknown to her.

Vice President Winslow, heavily rouged to distract from plastic surgery that hadn't gone well, hungered for the Presidency as she had all her life, and she remained a steadfast holdout. She'd put up with narcissistic President Gammon's wandering hands and his frequent belittlements despite her impressive qualifications as a former network news anchor. She wasn't about to resign with the presidency within reach at last. At a hastily assembled press conference, flanked by twelve Old Glory flags on poles, Winslow, waving her mic like a sword, noted that the U.S. Constitution was the only authority she'd ever bow to. Fists to the cameras, she asked for death before she'd lose liberty.

However, in a cleverly targeted warning following her press conference, Winslow learned the Selons had dissolved her makeup artist. That pushed her over the edge, and she resigned, followed by a trove of Cabinet heads and representatives. Reminding House Representatives that their exalted position gave them priority, Senators cut ahead of them in the race to the exit the U.S. Capital building.

America awaited its new leader.

4

ESCORTS

THWAP THWAP THWAP. Jeremiah opened an eye as the beat of helicopters over Madison, Georgia woke him from an unsettling dream to an unnerving reality.

The crash at his front door pried open his other eye. Marines wearing night vision headbands battered the door off splintered hinges and swarmed his house.

"Got him," the lead marine entered his bedroom.

Jeremiah stared in shock.

"Target secured," a second marine shouted.

"What? Jesus. What the hell …?" said Jeremiah, his voice an octave higher than usual, still half asleep as he took in the marines surrounding him, pistols drawn.

"Jeremiah Jeremy Butler?"

"Yes," said Jeremiah

"We need to leave immediately Sir. Quickly please," the first marine lifted goggles off his forehead and grabbed Jeremiah's arm.

"I haven't done anything," said Jeremiah.

"You're fine, but you have to come with us. Throw on pants and a shirt. We're out'a here."

"Jeremiah kicked off his covers, dressed, reached for the family Bible by his bedside, and left, the Marine leading his way.

Minutes later the beat of copter blades doubled then tripled in speed as three White Tops, Sikorsky VH-92As, two as decoys, lifted from his driveway. Jeremiah sat in Marine One between his Marine Corp escorts while the pilot confirmed over a secure comm band that they were in route.

Sleep-glaze lifting from his eyes, Jeremiah, pale, turned to the Marine at his side. "Could ya tell me what's going on. I don't fly. Scared to. Always have been, and this tin-can scares the bejesus out of me. I take trains and buses."

"You'll get used to it," said the Marine.

"Aren't you going to tell me? Am I under arrest? And what do y'all think I've done?" Jeremiah nervously tightened his seat straps. "Don't you have to read me my rights? Am I kidnapped? What makes you think I can pay?"

"Our orders are to secure you, Sir."

"I get a lawyer, right?"

"You'll be briefed once we're there."

"There? Where? This has to be a mistake. I'm a farmer, Jeremiah Jeremy Butler. Been home all night."

"We know that, Sir. General Hooker will explain once we're down."

Jeremiah shook his head, bewildered, nauseous and trying not to look outside. He touched the cross that hung from the chain on his neck and they flew on in silence.

"Holy mackerel," said Jeremiah as the copter descended. "Isn't that...." Marine One set in place with a bump.

"... the White House, Sir," said a Marine.

Marines hustled Jeremiah down rows of West Wing offices to the windowless Roosevelt Room. A massive oblong conference table dwarfed the room. Paintings of Theodore and Franklin D. Roosevelt were flanked by the Stars and Stripes and a blue Presidential seal flag.

Cabinet members waited, seated in high-back leather chairs around the table. Jeremiah eyed the stain on his overalls and felt the piercing stare of executives in suits and dresses. Though he couldn't place them all, he identified Averill McCain, the Secretary of Defense and Karrie Abrams from Homeland Security and Peter Luellen from Health and Human Services. It took a moment to place Charlie Miley who'd been President Gammon's Chief of Staff. The name finally came to him recalling Miley on the evening news when he announced, his voice choking with sobs, that President Gammon had succumbed to the virus. Miley ushered Jeremiah to the chair at the head of the conference table, but Jeremiah scanned for a less prominent seat and went for one against the wall. Miley motioned him back to the head.

Introducing himself as Chief of Staff, Miley handed the meeting over to General Hooker of the Joint Chiefs of Staff who in turn introduced the Cabinet members.

"Mr. Butler, Sir, do you know why you are here?" Miley asked.

"I ... well Sir ...," Jeremiah wiped his jeans, then stuffed hands down well-worn pockets, "Look ... I swear I didn't do what y'all think I did. I'm no terrorist or something, and I'd like to go home."

Several Cabinet members grinned.

"Sir, you're aware of the Selon broadcast? Their demands?" Miley asked.

"Who isn't," said Jeremiah. "Not much else on TV since that thing cut off my shows."

"Then you know we were compelled to conduct a lottery?" said Miley.

"Everyone knows it, yes Mr. Miley."

"And you know why the lottery was held?"

"To pick someone after President Gammon, may he rest in peace. It's all the press talks about. Word is, they held the drawing, but they never said who won."

"Actually, Sir, we just learned the name ourselves," said General Hooker leaning forward. His uniform was covered with multi-colored bars and his frame filled the executive chair. "Our first priority on learning was to secure the President-to-be. We kept the name in strict confidence of course - until we secured the new POTUS. Imagine the danger if word got out before we had him in a safe facility. Folks are angry enough about the Selons. The potential that he'd be harmed or kidnapped was high. But with the new POTUS secure, the Secret Service takes over now, with great thanks to the Marines," Hooker nodded to Marine General Abraham Trufow.

"Well Mr. Miley, when do we get to know," said Jeremiah, "the people, the press? Although I feel for the poor SOB, if you'll pardon my French.

He or she won't be popular. I don't know anybody who thinks the lottery's legit. Picking the president without an election. It's unAmerican."

"The rules have changed, I'm afraid," said Miley.

"And what's with these Selons?" said Jeremiah, "My neighbor said they're super-advanced? I hear they can make us do about anything? What's the deal, if it's okay that I ask?"

"Well, Sir, 'the deal' is that I'm afraid they can. The winning lottery number has been drawn, and the new President identified." Cabinet member again broke out in smiles. "And so that we don't risk angering the Selons, he's to assume the office immediately."

"He? So, it's a guy. I don't think the press knows that. Someone should tell them."

"You were selected, Sir."

"To tell the press? Don't you have people for that? Press secretaries? I wouldn't mind knowing who, though. A Democrat? Republican? From what state?"

"No, no. I mean, your name was drawn. Jeremiah Jeremy Butler," said Miley, looking down at his notes. "Your name was drawn. You will be the 56th President of the United States of America. President Jeremiah Jeremy Butler."

"Isn't this too important to joke about, Mr. Miley?"

"It's not a joke, Sir."

Jeremiah's face brightened. "Ahh, I get it now. Took me a while you guys, you. We Georgians aren't the sharpest pitchforks in the barn. This is one of those reality TV shows, right?" Jeremiah scanned for hidden cameras. "My daddy used to watch *Candid Camera* back in the fifties. It's like that, right? CBS? NBC? Cable?"

"This is serious, Mr. Butler," said General Hooker. "Why do you think we rushed you here? For your protection. It's time to inform the public. They need to know the country isn't leaderless."

"Come on. At least tell me the name of show."

General Hooker raised his eyebrows. "Despite tradition, the plan is to hold your swearing-in ceremony in private. We think it's wise to skip a formal inaugural – if you concur, of course. We recommend introducing you as America's new President by video – for your protection."

Jeremiah stared at his boots for what seemed an eternity.

"If you're not kidding, if this isn't a TV show, God help our country," said Jeremiah. "I can't think of anyone less qualified than me. I'm a black farmer, owner of a several thousand-acre farm, and proud of it. But a lottery? A black man. You folks know how well that goes over - though I have my birth certificate."

"The Selons made the rules, Sir, and it's you," said General Hooker.

"Make me president without an election? No way, I'm not your guy. I might offer the Department of Agriculture a few suggestions," said Jeremiah. "Way too much bureaucracy. The USDA has over 100,000 employees and for what?"

Secretary of Agriculture Hickory Jamal scowled.

"But this is way above my pay-grade," said Jeremiah. "You must have done a background check. You know any person in this room is better qualified. Madison, Georgia has 937 residents, and I never even ran for town council. I'm an American so I know almost nothing about government. Well, I can name the three branches. I read that seventy-four percent of Americans can't … that Annenberg study. My buddies at the grange can't name them: the Executive, Legislative, and Judicial, right? But for America's sake, get somebody qualified. Substitute anyone who makes sense and announce it. Who'd ever know?"

"The Selon's would, Sir, and they won't permit deviation."

"Jesus," Jeremiah put his head in his hands. "This can't be happening."

"It's understandable that you doubt your ability, Sir," said Miley. "Even if you were experienced, who in their right mind wouldn't be afraid? It's healthy, and if you'll permit me to say so, it's a novelty to see someone come to the White House who admits they're not competent. But you'll have tremendous support. The folks in this room are here for you – and many others."

The room filled with polite assent.

"You'll have experts in every area and 2.1 million federal employees to back you up."

Jeremiah looked down the long, polished conference table, avoiding the eyes staring at him. "I'm worried you people are serious," he said, thinking, *I don't have a clue. Who do I trust? I see the news. Powerful people make demands on the President, and no matter what the poor bastard does, someone is out to get him."*

"I have no idea what's important …," said Jeremiah.

"… you'll get briefed as soon as you take the oath," said General Hooker.

"The oath? Of Office? I just found out."

"Chief Justice Sweindoffer will preside. Any Bible preference?" said Hooker.

"Holy I guess," said Jeremiah.

"You can use The George Washington Inaugural Bible if you wish. Or a family bible. Roosevelt and John Quincy Adams didn't use a bible, but we're told you're a churchgoer. At the risk of sounding pedantic, for the past two hundred years taking the Oath of Office has assured citizens of the continuity of American leadership – of a peaceful transition."

"Are you sure the Selons want a peaceful transition?" said Jeremiah. "I hear all kinds of things. And when do you want me to take the Oath, surely you don't mean today?"

"Yes this afternoon, Sir. It's important. Making it a *fait accompli* will muzzle the legal challenges that are coming."

Jeremiah's eyes glazed. His Cabinet gave him time. Finally, Jeremiah pulled his hands from his jeans and spoke, "This Oath. It happens here in the White House? Can somebody show me where?"

"With your approval, Sir, given the circumstance of your transition, we thought a private ceremony in the south portico of the White House is wise. In 1945, Franklin D. Roosevelt chose that venue for his Oath," he nodded to the painting.

"Jesus." Jeremiah paled. "Suppose there's a crisis – a run on the banks. More floods?"

"Immediately following the swearing in," said Miley, "you'll get your first PDB … Presidential Daily Briefing."

5

ACRONYMS

JEREMIAH BUTLER STOOD at the window overlooking the South Lawn. His view from the Oval blurred as if peering through cellophane and his head throbbed. Hours of preparatory briefings and following lasers across organizational charts took a toll. How many times had he gone over the White House organizational tree with boxes showing titles and roles of Cabinet department officers? The size of his White House staff staggered him. He'd had no idea – eighteen hundred strong and a budget of nearly $750 million. Maybe his GOP buddies had a point about bloated government.

He'd asked Miley to block some alone time – saying he needed to digest the charts of the bureaucracy that imprisoned him. But what he really needed was an hour, even a half hour, of private time when he didn't have to pump hands or respond energetically. Constant social contact depleted Jeremiah to the point where every cell in his body seemed to plead for silence – space to recharge before the next onslaught of high-powered executives with requests related to unfamiliar subjects. He thought of his dad. People, crowds energized his father, but they sucked him dry.

Moving to Washington from Madison, Georgia had been disorienting. He arrived like a foreigner, quickly learning Washingtonians had a language all their own and he didn't speak it. It magnified his sense of inadequacy. Each department chief that passed through the Oval had a title followed by a string of acronyms that whizzed by like a biplane banner - 'OMB', 'OEM', 'GSA', 'HUD', 'DOT', 'SBA', 'FCC'. Even the capital city, not so long ago a quaint southern town, was an acronym.

Jeremiah's befuddlement was obvious to eye-rolling advisors whose names he forgot after meeting them. It didn't help that they dressed uniformly - men in pinstriped suits with power ties and handkerchiefs folded to a pocket point; balayage blonde women with overly firm handshakes. He felt uncomfortable in the stiff suit tailors brought and constantly loosened the tie that felt like a hangman's noose - longing for his well-worn overalls and scuffed boots. He told himself that he'd better get used to the White House dress code after overhearing staff mimic his 'y'all'.

Jeremiah rested his head on the historic Resolute, feeling out-of-element at the ornate desk, an 1880 gift from Queen Victoria to Rutherford B. Hayes. Chief of Staff Miley explained the Queen ordered it fashioned from thirteen-hundred pounds of oak salvaged from the British Arctic exploration ship, the *HMS Resolute*.

He'd wondered about the circular design of his office. The Oval, Miley explained, traced back to 1791 when George Washington wanted the room's straight rear walls refashioned to form the circle-shaped Blue room – deemed a more imposing venue for the first President to greet international guests. In 1909 Taft ordered a southwest extension, accomplished by no less than the renowned architect Nathan C. Wyeth.

Jeremiah swiveled in the tall leather chair and scanned the room, pausing on sculptures of Rosa Parks and Abraham Lincoln, and on portraits of Franklin Delano Roosevelt and Benjamin Franklin. The art added to the musk of ceremony that burdened him. Like the unknown narrator in "The Pit and the Pendulum," he felt trapped as if the walls closed in and in the tortuously slow fashion Poe described.

I can't do this, Jeremiah thought. *I'm no bureaucrat. I like my meetings in the fields with my team. Stick me in my old Allis-Chalmers, and me and my guys will get a field cleared lickey-split. Charts are all they grow here.* He dug for a pinch of Red Man, pressing a fresh plug between cheek and gums, closing his eyes to savor juice that offered distraction.

I could try to slip away tonight. But I'm never out of their sight. It's a wonder the Secret Service hasn't stationed an agent in my bed with the covers pulled up to his lapel mic.

He lifted his head. *What if I ask them to run me home - say I need a few things from the farm. I could excuse myself for the bathroom and slip out the back window. If I could make it past the granary, I could head for the falls in Oconee National Forest.*

He shook his head. *Who am I kidding? Even if I gave them the slip, in minutes they'll have teams crawling the woods. I'm a prisoner and the Selons made sure my only option is to do this job or get zapped to pixels.*

What do they think I can accomplish? I can't find my way through the White House corridors let alone deal with the planet's chaos. What good is my Penn State B.S. in Agribusiness Management when these folks have Harvard degrees and make sure I know it. Show me a row of failing wheat, and I'll tell you what the land needs. But this? The only thing I know about government is from high school civics - which schools don't even teach anymore.

Jeremiah spit tobacco juice into a brass spittoon the White House Curator found for him. It had been stationed in the halls of Congress years ago.

I'm caged, the sharks are circling, and I'm chum to attract them. Can I trust anyone? Chief of Staff Miley seems on my side. I Googled him and he's an attorney whose been around D.C. for years. But power-trippers sprout like pigweed in the West Wing.

He glanced at his watch and closed his eyes. *Five more minutes before they make me practice my speech for the 'eighty-seventh' time.*

6

STATE OF THE UNION

THE HOUSE CHAMBER hushed as the nine Supreme Court justices entered followed by the President's Cabinet less the Designated Survivor. At the entrance the Sargent at Arms bellowed the eight words that have introduced President's since 1790:

"Mister Speaker. The President of the United States."

Every president had delivered the constitutionally mandated annual assessment, the 'Annual Message' until Franklin Roosevelt when it became the 'State of the Union' address - with two exceptions: William Henry Harrison and James Garfield. Both died before they had a chance to deliver one.

Jeremiah Jeremy Butler entered the chamber. The few tepid claps ceased when representatives realized other legislators denied the new president the traditional courtesy. The few who welcomed him stopped and worried that TV cameras could have captured them clapping. The House Chamber, capable of holding fourteen hundred, wasn't full as several loudly boycotted an address from a 'hijacked' presidency.

President Jeremiah Butler walked down the carpeted isle with no hands outstretched. He ascended the speaker's platform in pin drop silence. Though reporting to the nation was mandatory, neither the Vice President nor the Speaker of the House acknowledged him from their lofty seats. As scripted, Jeremiah extended his hand, but neither took it. He turned to the podium, the chamber's silence broken only by an occasional cough.

"Mister Speaker, the Vice President, Members of Congress, my fellow Americans," President Butler began. He'd worked with White House

speech coaches for weeks to practice his delivery, learning to enunci-
ate - when to emphasize - when to pause and gesture - to maintain eye
contact with his audience as well as the TV cameras while following the
scrolling teleprompter. A linguist helped suppress his rural vernacular.

The first rehearsal had Chief of Staff Miley in a panic. But Jeremiah
improved, determined not to embarrass himself or the American people,
and after a few sessions the tightness in Miley's gut eased.

Jeremiah rested hands on the podium and looked up at the
teleprompter, a technology not available in the days of Roosevelt's fireside
chats. Jeremiah's nod signaled for the teleprompter to scroll, but the text
stayed fixed on the page until the screen went blank. Jeremiah banged
the teleprompter as one might pound a flickering TV set, then searched
the chamber for Miley who was gesturing emphatically to a group of
technicians. Silence dominated the chamber as the audience waited. A
few began drumming fingers. Jeremiah labored to smile as he retrieved
the hard copy from his suit pocket. But as he straightened the pages,
the text disappeared. Whispers grew to a buzz, and coughs came like
popcorn.

Buying time, Butler took a slow sip of water, frantically debating. *I
could walk away, but they'll call me a quitter, and I'll be humiliated. I could
try it from memory. That could be a disaster.*

Terror beat his chest while he considered. He sucked in a deep breath
and chose to wing it. *This might be a train wreck.*

Watching from his position light-years away in the furthest ring of the
Milky Way Galaxy, Commander Gregor concentrated intently on the
Earthling at the podium as President Butler's teleprompter went dark.
Gregor focused on the text in Jeremiah's hard copy and it too vanished.
Quivering with excitement, he watched Jeremiah flounder. *Your speech
disappeared, did it, Mr. President?* Gregor beamed. *Such a shame. Going
to try to ad lib it, are you? Have at it, Mr. Chief Executive. Fall flat on your
homo sapiens face, and maybe Eminence will wake up and let my team get
on with finishing off another of the galaxies' utterly useless species.*

"My ... fellow Americans," Jeremiah looked up. *Well, I got that right.*
"Most in this room know William Zillon and for Americans at home he

was President's Gammon's brilliant speechwriter." Jeremiah waved blank pages. "Bill helped me write what I wanted to say tonight. But I've decided to throw our speech away, and just say what's on my mind." He set the speech on the podium, paused and faced the chamber.

"You didn't choose me. There was no election. And yes, I was forced on you. But least you forget, the Presidency was forced on me in case you think I relish this."

A few in the chamber gasped. Candor in a State of the Union address was unprecedented.

"I watch the six-o-clock news and see many of you on TV," Jeremiah pointed to his audience. "I know some of you would die to switch places with me. The presidency is your life ambition, and I get that you're furious that some guy had it handed to him – a Georgia farmer with zero Washington experience who doesn't want to be here. And okay … a black man. But I am here, and there's nothing you or I can do but accept it. We've seen what happens to folks who deny a Selon mandate. Poof," Jeremiah made a cloud with his hands.

"When General Hooker told me my name was drawn, to be honest I thought the Selons were … ahh … well, nuts." Jeremiah eyed the ceiling. "But as the days went on, I got to thinking. Maybe it's an opportunity?"

Mutters from chamber seats.

"You doubt that, sure. But I don't need years in Washington to know we're in trouble. I watch the six o'clock news. The oceans are flooding us. My farm's a mud pit. Forget 'amber waves of grain'. My wheat reeks of brine, and food's scarce. Mother nature must be in a wicked bad mood, because in addition to her floods, we have pandemics. The Yellow Plague cut down the man who ought to be up here – our properly elected leader, President Gammon, may his soul rest in peace. But he's gone.

"I can't recall times this hard. I nearly missed my mortgage payment … until Miley said how much they pay me now. And the checks come like clockwork. But many of my buddies back in Madison don't have work.

"Did I mention wars … America has soldiers all over the globe.

"Okay that's enough half-empty glass talk, but we have to face where we are.

"You don't want to hear this, but I can't figure out many of you in this room. I hear you on TV talking as if things are fine, but you know they aren't, and the American people know it. My dad used to say ... 'If it walks like one and quacks like one ... admit it's a duck.'

"Which brings me to the Selons. I'm told they're highly advanced. But in any case, they're running the show. You may not like this, but I agree with some of the things that avatar said. So resign yourself that it won't be business as usual."

The room filled with muttering.

"We brought Earth to this point, you and I, not the Selons. It's a mess with our name on it."

Hisses.

"... so maybe lookin' fresh at what we've done – why government doesn't work anymore – is a good thing.

"Me and my buddies in Madison used to meet for coffee mornings and talk about you. We see bickering, elbowing, power-grabbing, but we don't see much getting done. The roads up my way have sink holes, the bridge past my farm is unsafe, and the Hard Labor Creek Regional Reservoir walls are crumbling. All your committee meetings haven't fixed them. And calling each other 'fascists' and 'socialists' isn't getting my bridge done.

"You the expert now?" yelled a representative from Missouri.

Butler paused and stared him down. "Look congressman. If I fail, you fail. The Selons made clear that it's time to make hard choices. We're talking survival.

"Until now, being as powerful as you in this room meant you'd be okay even in tough times - whether or not you got anything done. You just had to get reelected.

"But times are bad now. Kids are hungry for God's sake ... in the United States of America. Students leave college neck-high in debt and can't find jobs. In Los Angeles and even in little Madison, Georgia, the city streets are lined with folks peeking out of cardboard boxes. Some are on drugs, and some are there 'cause they're sick and surgery costs too much. Medicine's broken and we've dropped down the list of countries that provide good care. We don't even live as long.

"I've only been here a few months, but I watch how you spend your day. You're busy hitting up the folks that got you here – and it's not entirely your fault since elections have become about dialing-for-dollars."

A senator stood, gestured thumbs down and noisily left the chamber.

"When do we address what people need? When I farm, it's not enough to think about what I'll plant for the next harvest. The boys and I talk about the right crops so the soil stays rich for the harvest after that, and even the season that follows.

"Thinking past reelection won't be easy. Do you think I don't get how hard you worked to earn a seat in this chamber? I can't imagine how many hands you shook; how many one-percenters you had to hit up; how many boring cocktail parties you dragged yourself to when there was a good game on. And yes, even the times you had to blink at legislation you knew wasn't right."

"Nearly done?" shouted a congressman.

"And that kind of stuff needs to stop," said Jeremiah shaking a finger.

It took him a moment to unclench his fist before continuing. "We work together, or die together. And if we fail, it's not just about us; it's 'lights out' for families, for kids, for Earth itself. Anyone here who doesn't get that? Could the Selons make it any clearer?"

The room returned to pin drop silence.

"When my dad started our farm forty years ago, he hung a Confucius saying on his wall:

If we don't change direction, we're likely to end up where we're headed.

"When you go home tonight and lie in bed, ask if it's gonna' be business as usual. If so, I'd like you to imagine you're looking at a photograph from the future. Imagine it's a Selon family vacationing here on Earth, and their kid finds a bone fossil in the dirt. It'll be quite the archaeological discovery when it's identified as the remains of the last homo sapiens.

"Help me, will you. Write bills that solve problems. Yes, it will anger your donors. CEOs will be angry that you made choices they don't like. But that's what leaders do. Think Pearl Harbor and how Americans dug in together."

Impatient rustling.

"I'm almost done."

The first claps of the evening.

"But one last thing."

Groans.

"I look out the window in the Oval and think about how, after winning the lottery, they brought me here. That same day, with my hand on our old family Bible, Chief Justice Sweindoffer administered the oath of office. I had to make a pledge. Tonight I'm taking a second oath.

"I swear as your president – when they bring me a bill, I don't care who I anger or please. It'll be thumbs up if the bill gets things around here moving ... down if it doesn't ... whatever the consequences.

"I'll screw up. From what I've seen in my short time here, simple answers are scarce as hen's teeth. You help one group, you hurt another. Someone loves you, and someone's angry. If once-upon-a-time our job was easy, that time is gone. But we must give it our best. I pledge that to you, and hope you'll do the same."

"Finished preaching?" hollered a representative.

"Yes, and thanks for hearing me out," said the President.

"Finally," came a shout.

"May the good Lord bless you and bless America," said Jeremiah, "and protect our precious Earth."

Jeremiah stepped from the podium, and walked out. The silence was funereal.

■■■

From his place high atop the Milky Way Galaxy, Commander Gregor tuned in on the thoughts of the representatives and found their rage delicious.

7

LIGHT ON THE SUBJECT

"**M**Y POINT IS that Butler ...

"... I reviewed the archives on State of the Union speeches," Gregor interrupted Darius, "... you're aware that Jeremiah Butler got the lowest approval rating ever polled. They hate him and many boycotted the event entirely. Several that didn't stood and gave him a thumbs down. Others interrupted with shouts, and one walked out mid-speech.

"William Jefferson Clinton, the 42nd American president, droned on for an hour and twenty-eight minutes of rambling self-congratulation. His audience dozed, but they didn't wish him dead. Congress greeted Butler in dead silence – not even perfunctory applause, and they were scowling when he left. Eminence has to see that humans won't work with a leader foisted on them ... especially one as unfamiliar with the ways of the District as Jeremiah Butler, a farmer."

"He needs time, Gregor," said Darius. "If you were more of an empath, you'd understand their reaction. They've been raised on the myth that elections reflect the people's will. They're not inquisitive enough to discover that fake news, foreign hacking, gerrymandered districts and voter suppression put presidents in office."

"I'm no expert on primitives," said Gregor, "but I don't have to walk on fours to know Butler doesn't have a chance. Progress would require that the representatives confront the special interests that got them to Washington. They won't. They're too preoccupied with pandering to their base to deal with a government that isn't functional."

"You say you don't understand them, Gregor, yet you judge them before Seer's completes the test," said Darius.

"Because it's a forgone conclusion. Do you really expect them to follow a president who comes without blue chip affiliations? Name one traditional power block that supports him. He lacks ties to the corporations that own the American presidency. Then too, there's his genetics."

"Meaning?"

"The tan."

"What about 'the tan'?"

"The Speaker of the House calls him 'the Nigger'."

"I've heard a few in Congress use the word in private, but it baffles me," said Darius.

"It's easy enough to understand. With homo sapiens, skin tone is a primary determinant of status," said Gregor. "The lighter the skin, the higher the status. Social status is defined by their irrational pecking order: they rank by skin-tone, celebrity, wealth - or great debt, religious affiliation, and political allegiance – in that order."

"But skin-tone?" said Darius.

"Nothing new," said Gregor. "They fixate on epidermal pigmentation, not intellect or physical prowess. Europeans who settled in North America hated the native skin color because it differed from theirs. Called the natives 'redskins'. The importance given to skin-tone grew in the early sixteen-hundreds with slavery. American blacks found it lucrative to imprison blacks captured from Africa. They chained them on ships and sold any who survived for crop slaves. Whites bought them at markets, considered them part of their portfolio, and justified slavery as the 'kindly protection of ignorant animals'. Blacks who rebelled were lynched … more than four thousand were hung. Lynching provided a festive social event for whites who found it entertaining to watch people swing."

"Barbaric," said Darius, "but give them credit. They ended slavery."

"Did they? Northern whites piously proposed an end to slavery, but their dispute with slave owners led to embittered war. The Northern victory emancipated the slaves so long as there was general agreement they'd remain second-class. As to the slave owners, The District of Columbia Compensated Emancipation Act offered them up to $300 a slave as reparations."

"But slavery did end," said Darius.

31

"Did it? The plantation owners still needed labor, and since ownership of one human by another was now outlawed, they hired back their former slaves at subsistence wages. Slavery continued but was renamed and called 'labor'. Poor whites joined poor blacks to celebrate their 'freedom' to work slave-like hours for twelve to fourteen daily, holding two and even three jobs so they could shelter and feed their families. It's still that way in many agricultural towns. Here, have a look." Gregor flashed a screen before Darius. "Migrant pickers in the fields of Immokalee, Florida work from sunrise to sunset to earn $10,000 to $15,000 a year. It's illegal to beat them, but do they work less hard than a plantation slave? The poverty rate is 43.4%."

"Well, the lynchings stopped," said Darius.

"Or were they were also rebranded? Rather than let unruly mobs hang slaves, the white-skins recruited a militia of eight hundred thousand enforcement officers and trained them as warriors to enforce what they call 'law and order'. They don't hang; they shoot blacks disproportionately."

"Not true, Gregor," said Darius.

"Isn't it? There were 1,056 recorded killings by police in Earth year 2021. And to help maintain the elite, the population armed itself with over four hundred million guns, 98% of which are in civilian hands. The species is a galactic blemish."

"What's your thing against humans, Gregor? I can point to a hundred Galactic societies with brutal pecking orders," said Darius. "We haven't interfered with them, and some are stranger than humans. Take the Pretorians of Planet Nine who worship citizens with putrid breath."

"I'd hate to be a Pretorian dentist," said Gregor.

"I'll pass on that too, Gregor. But why does basing class on skin-tone bother you more than the other irrational hierarchies in the galaxy?" said Darius.

"Because the way humans segregate by skin-color is so illogical," said Gregor.

"How's that?" said Darius.

"Come on Darius, you were with the team that mapped Xonium deposits along Earth's ocean coasts. What did you see? Here, let me refresh your memory." The screen appeared again, this time showing a

California beach with humans basking in droves on blankets along the shore.

"So? They're resting. On holiday. Basking half naked in Sol, their sun star," said Darius.

"What do you think they're doing, Darius? Trying to darken their skin. Get blacker," said Gregor. "They call it 'tanning'."

"You mean they strive for lower status?" said Darius.

"That's the oddity. If dark skin comes from the beach, it raises status." said Gregor as the screen dissolved.

"Are you serious?" said Darius.

"If you're looking for logic among them, you'll be a while," said Gregor. "They operate by instinct but call it science. For how many centuries did they insist their Earth was flat?

"The Babylonians thought the earth was hollow with an underworld just below the surface. The Egyptians saw it as a four-cornered square. Aristotle argued Earth must be spherical because it left a curved shadow on the moon during an eclipse, and sailors reported that ship masts in the distance would sink below the horizon. True to form, the scientists of Aristotle's day ignored him."

"Be fair Gregor. How about Pythagoras, and Archimedes, and Euclid. All thoughtful men," said Darius. "And homo sapiens science has evolved."

"A bit, but the predominant instinct is to cover their eyes when a need for change is obvious. You saw them tune out when our avatar listed the threats facing Earth. Did they listen with an open mind as any Selon would? I don't know what you see in them, Darius, but I'm meeting with Parliament to ask them to reconsider and let me bring my team to Earth."

8

THE APPEAL

"COMMANDER GREGOR, YOU'VE come to petition Parliament about the test? Again?" said Eminence,

"I have," said Gregor, "As those assembled know, I head up elimination in the Milky Way Galaxy's fourth quadrant where my teams just returned from eradicating two of the species under Parliament's watchful eye. Eradication of the homo sapiens was to be next, but the Overseers issued a hold. Provost Darius convinced them to test for some vague potential he sees in them."

"We know this, Commander Gregor," said Eminence.

"Darius insists he's found humans who are rational, compassionate and place community over self interest. I've explained that occasional benevolence is a genetic aberration, but greed is more characteristic of human nature. If Parliament agrees, I wish to complete my assignment."

"Seer's test stems from the Overseer's desire to obey the Prime Directive. Yet here you go again, Gregor, petitioning us to override it." said Eminence.

"Because the expanding universe strains my resources and necessitates efficiency," said Gregor. "When I see a species with little capacity to care for itself and with minimal regard for its planet, I don't need a test. In the long run swift action is the way to honor the Prime Directive. We can't be everywhere and debate about each of a million species."

"Yet the Overseer's instructions are clear. Provost Darius successfully argued that man has evolved - that humans today are kinder and gentler than, say, the great empire of the Aztecs who had to feed their sun god Huitzilopochtli with human hearts and blood. The Overseers instructed us to test so unless you have something new, it's your presence here, Commander, that's an inefficient use of our time."

"But I come with new evidence," said Gregor.

"Oh?"

"The human picked by your lottery now leads the Americans."

"Hardly news, Gregor. That's all you have?"

"And recently the tribe's leaders assembled to hear him speak."

"Also things we know," said Eminence.

"But instead of impressing his audience, Butler infuriated the representatives ... even the one who came with an open mind," said Gregor. "I'm here to tell you that Jeremiah Butler bungled his State of the Union speech, and his incompetence united Congress against him."

"What did you expect, Gregor? Did you think those congressmen and senators would welcome a president not installed by a big donor? Every species fights us initially and the acquiesces out of fear, It gives Butler time to make progress, but you don't want to hear that, do you Gregor?" said Eminence.

"Butler's delivery at the State of the Union was one fumble after another," said Gregor.

"And of course you had nothing to do with that, Gregor?" said Eminence. "Provost Darius told us of your, shall we say, assistance with his teleprompter."

Gregor ignored the comment. "Butler's a farmer. Bureaucrats never want a leader with hands soiled by work."

"He faces challenges," said Eminence.

"Farmers have no status with homo sapiens... and a black one..."

"Look Gregor...,"said Eminence.

"... your test will show," Gregor spoke over Eminence, "that there is no future for a species that can't get past self interest."

"That's your conviction, Gregor, but you act like it's proven fact," said Eminence.

"Then let me offer fact. Do you know what was being planned even while Butler addressed Congress? Earthlings are unaware that we monitor thought."

"Proceed," said Eminence.

"When I mind-tapped Senator Julius Napalie from Missouri, here's what was he was planning."

I'll be god-dammed if that arrogant nigger ever gets support from me – the hayseed puppet. I'll filibuster every bill he supports."

"Good luck making progress with Napalie around," said Gregor. "And there's more …"
"Continue," said Eminence.
"More serious than Senator Napalie's threat is what Avril Thermadore, the Speaker of the House, was thinking."

"When the committee comes by the house tonight, we'll settle on how to gut Butler. We'll make sure he doesn't finish his term. With the Yellow Pandemic spreading, who would suspect us if Butler gets so ill he can't preform his duties. Or dies. The new VP resigns - now there's someone who follows orders. Let's see what the boys say tonight."

"Given what Thermadore was thinking, we already have the test result," said Gregor. "Talented or inept, weak or strong – it doesn't matter what Jeremiah Butler offers. Congress isn't listening."
"I'll grant you that Congress isn't burdened by open minds. Darius attributes it to an electoral process that favors deeply narcissistic leaders. But he's shown us there are compassionate leaders also. Our test will weigh the preponderance of those extremes. If nothing else, it'll be a useful addition to the Galaxy's research archives."
"But..."
"Petition denied, Gregor. The test goes on. We'll have plenty of time for your services if and when they are needed."
"*When*," said Gregor.

9

THE OVAL

"Majority Leader Erling Claymore and Senator Tobias Madrid for their appointment, Mr. President."

"The two you spoke of, Miley?"

"Yes, Sir."

"Remind me."

"Hear them out but don't commit when they press for your veto," said Miley moving for the door.

"Miley," Leader Erling Claymore passed Miley without looking.

"Have a seat, Senators." President Butler motioned. "Can I offer you coffee? Something stronger?"

"Thanks, Mr. President," said Leader Claymore, taking ownership of the couch. "Nothing with hair on it before ten."

"I wouldn't mind a Scotch, neat," said Senator Madrid.

"Well then," said the President leaning forward, "Miley tells me your committee had quite a session yesterday. Been a year since I took office, but they say it was more contentious than anything during my term so far."

"It was heated," said Madrid, flicking a speck of dandruff from his Brioni. "We deadlocked on the bills - split right down the middle. We'd like to talk about that, Mr. President."

"How can I help, Senators?"

"Thank you, Mr. President. So, getting right to it, HR-1 is a terrible bill, but with your support we can kill it," said Leader Claymore. "Senator Rawlings' bill would revert districts it took us years to reshape. It'll hurt us in the midterms … you as well. We're still having midterms? Have the Selons said so?"

"As best I know we're having them," said the President. "I can't say so with certainty – but so far they haven't interfered."

"You're here," said Madrid.

"Yes Senator and we can all agree that I wouldn't be President but for them. But I am President, so I suggest you get past that. But about the bills. They seem reasonable to me. Chief of Staff Miley says that HR-1 limits geographic manipulation in elections. To quote him, the President reached for a paper on his desk, "'Districts would be shaped solely by mathematical aggregation, eliminating efforts to accommodate party bias'."

"The district borders are fine as we set them," said Madrid.

"Miley said you've gerrymandered them," said Butler.

"To obtain the advantage we need in the primaries. You should want that too. Rawlings' bill would limit our ability to control who runs against who," said Leader Claymore.

President Butler crossed his arms, "Shouldn't the voters determine that?"

Madrid smiled. "That's a nice way to think of it, Mr. President. You're talking proportional representation - winning seats based on nothing more than who gets the most votes. But we don't do things that way anymore. The popular vote became less important decades ago. Five American Presidents assumed office without winning the popular vote, most recently Gore vs. Bush and Clinton vs. Trump. Of course your own presidency bypassed voting completely."

Butler ignored the comment. "But isn't fiddling with district boundaries putting your finger on the scale?"

"I wouldn't say so. Gerrymandering dates to 1812 and Vice President Elbridge Gerry, a man I've long admired. A leader who knew how to keep his allies. I never understood why the history books give him so little mention," said Leader Claymore.

"But at the end of the day, gerrymandering weakens democracy," said the President.

"The framers never intended for the populace to elect our leaders which is why there's an electoral college – to limit the influence of the inexperienced - begging your pardon," said Leader Claymore.

The President bit his lip.

"HR-1 would strip us of the best weapon we have against opponents, and it'll be doubly valuable with the new census out. That always provides low hanging fruit to give us an edge," said Senator Madrid.

"Gentlemen, I don't have your years of experience," said the President. "But gerrymandering has leaders picking voters, and it's supposed to be the other way around. Weaken voters and power concentrates at the top. Isn't that how we got a musclebound legislature that routinely stalemates. The lottery put me here to shake things up, and gerrymandering makes it harder," Butler paused to spit into his spittoon. "Miley says that HR-1 will swing the pendulum back and facilitate change."

"Change. Change. Change. It rarely leads to progress," said Leader Claymore. "If Democrats are back in power, what does change get us? Out-of-control spending, budget deficits, a trade imbalance - chaos," he shook a finger at the President.

"He's right," said Madrid, "and if Claymore and I lose our seats, Democrats will do what they always do - dump money into the safety net. They cut taxes which increases the deficit. They defund the police, siphon off military spending so folks on the dole get more. People get dependent on government, unemployment soars, the economy tanks," Madrid, pantomimed a crash with a diving hand.

"But gerrymandering…" said the President.

"…is our safety net," said the Leader interrupting the President. "Packing and cracking are as American as Old Glory."

"Packing? Cracking?" said the President.

"Cracking. We split voters into new districts – send those off who don't support us," said Claymore.

"How does that help?" said the President.

"Well for example, voters in an urban area can be reapportioned to suburban districts. You get voters more favorable to you. I owe my seat to an algorithm," said Leader Claymore.

"Hijacking and kidnapping are vital too," said Senator Madrid, "but HR-1 threatens that."

"I'm afraid you need to define them as well," said the President.

Senator Madrid began speaking very, very slowly. "Well … Mr. President … imagine … you're up against … two super-popular opponents. You hijack their districts. That is, you redraw them and force the two to run against each other. One loses whereas without hijacking, both might win."

"Kidnapping," added Claymore, "is moving an incumbent's district into a less favorable population."

"Quite the plan," said the President.

"A sure-fire primary-booster. That's why you have to veto both HR-1 and HR-2. Assuming the Selons will permit a veto? You're their guy, right?" said Leader Claymore.

"I'm hardly 'their guy', Claymore," said the President, "and as I said, they don't talk to me. But that avatar implied we have one last chance to get government to show results. My administration and both of you need to help dig us out of this hole."

"Will they let us?" said Madrid.

"My take on them is that your job as legislators matters as much as ever … though I haven't seen much legislating other than renaming post offices which you're really good at. Almost 20% of enacted legislation has been renaming post offices."

Leader Claymore scowled.

"From what I see, each side of the isle blocks the other," said the President. "If HR-1 gives the people more say, it could break the stalemate."

"May I be blunt?" said Senator Madrid.

"Candor is rare in the Oval but welcome5t," said the President.

"That 'will of the people' stuff," said Madrid making air quotes, "that's not how things work now. Government stopped fiddle-fucking with the masses years ago. The public wants handouts - a slippery slope to socialism."

"Shouldn't government serve them, Madrid? 'Of the people, for the people'? The President made air quotes back at him.

"I'm all for the people. I stand behind the constitution and love Democracy. Come to my office someday and see the painting behind my desk – a mosaic with all 27 versions of Old Glory - every American flag from the Betsy Ross to each new flag as we added a state. But my job – and yours if I may say so – is to keep the wrong folks out of Congress - to be sure our kind stays in power which ensures everyone's prosperity," said Madrid. "That's the real 'for the people'."

"If only it were true Madrid," said the President. "But your first words this morning were that your committee is stalemated again."

"And we break the logjam by winning a more viable majority," said Claymore. "Killing HR-1 makes that happen."

"Bottom line for me, Senators, is that we have bridges to fix, and kids that need school lunches and the carbon load to address. Yet back in Madison, I didn't see it happening," said the President.

Claymore looked at Madrid and raised his eyebrows.

"If that's what you want, you need to help kill HR-2 also," said Madrid. "Rawlings' bill makes it harder to disqualify voters."

"How's that done?" said the President.

"At present, a small discrepancy – say in a name or address - lets us bounce them off the rolls or deny them a mail-in."

"But why would you want to?" said the President.

"Take Pennsylvania's 13th district. It's 93.1% white. Law of averages says we want every vote. But the 5th congressional district is different. It's loaded with folks of a different lineage - so you want every challenge," said Madrid.

The President listened expressionless.

"In a blue district like the 5th,' said Madrid, "say a voter's driver's license reads 'Jose A. Rodriguez', but his registration card reads 'Jose Rodriguez' or 'Jose Alejandro Rodriguez'. We'd send him home, but HR-2 makes it harder."

"I see, Tobias, and I believe Miley said HR-2 has provisions directing how a state certifies the vote?"

"HR-2 cuts off our legs there too," said Madrid. "Presently after we canvass, if we don't like the tally but the Secretary of State is set to certify, we can replace him or her," said Claymore. "We get the result we want."

"You stay in power."

"Exactly. Leaving things alone assures the right outcome," said Madrid.

President Butler stood up.

"So, can we count on you?" said Leader Claymore rising also, and turning to face to the President.

"One more thing, Senators," the President sidestepped Claymore. "Miley mentioned term limits?"

"Very important, Mr. President. HR-11 proposes term limits, but a veto from you assures that nothing can take away our seats. Well, nothing but death. We haven't solved that one yet," said Madrid fist-bumping Claymore.

"Nor have the Selons," smiled President Butler, "though they live a lot longer."

"So we can count on your vetoes, Mr. President?" said Leader Claymore moving in on the President.

The room quieted.

"I need time, Senators. Minority leader Rawlings asked to meet, and I'd like to get the thinking from both sides of the isle. I'll get back to you. This meeting clarifies a lot."

"Of course, Mr. President. But careful with Rawlings. He's partisan," said Madrid, setting his glass on the table.

"I'll expect to hear from you," said Leader Erling Claymore exiting.

10

A Republic ... If

SENATOR CREEDENCE RAWLINGS' burly hand dwarfed the demitasse as he gulped. "The way I see it, Mr. President, Ben Franklin nailed it when on leaving the Constitutional Convention he was asked what kind of government they'd formed. 'A Republic ... if you can keep it,' Franklin said. We're here about keeping it. To ask you to sign HR-1, HR-2 and HR-11 if they pass."

"That's why we've come," said Congressman Gillmoe Jillings. His brow wrinkled as he turned to Senator Rawlings, "My constituents don't like it called a 'Republic.'"

"Let's focus on the bills, Jillings," said Rawlings.

Having savored the last, spent dregs of chaw juice, President Jeremiah Butler leaned over his spittoon, then offered the open tin. "A plug, gentlemen?"

Rawlings turned away, "My sweet tooth is vice enough."

"I'm a Wild Turkey guy," said Jillings looking for a bar cart.

The President smiled, turning to Senator Rawlings. "On *Meet the People* you talked about your voting rights legislation."

"My bill limits how they manipulate districts," said Rawlings. "Gerrymandering corrals voters in a way that's undemocratic to the core."

"HR-1 does that? In my short time in office I've seen a load of tricks to stifle voters - death by a thousand legislative cuts," said the President

Jillings eyed his watch. "Any bourbon?" he asked.

The President looked at Rawlings to measure his reaction. "I'll have some fetched Congressman. So what's the answer, Senator?"

"When Congress grows too powerful, we become less and less responsive to the people," said Rawlings. "Rather than address their needs, we spend our time creating moats around our authority. Just as the Selon said, we won't address Earth's crisis until we break the hold of those with a lock on power. It won't be easy."

"No small understatement that," said the President.

"May I be blunt about what's needed?" said Rawlings.

"Please," the President nodded.

"We both know folks are angry about how you got here, and they keep bickering about it. I'm a glass half-full kind of guy, and I see the Butler Presidency as a chance to shake up representative government. Right now most of what Congress does is protect the status quo. The Butler administration is our second chance if we take it."

The President turned and faced Rawlings. "Let me ask you Senator - suppose the lottery drew your name. What would your priority be if other than keeping your seat?"

Senator Rawlings paused. "Well ... the brilliance of the founding fathers is undeniable, but the constitution doesn't self-correct to preserve their intent. It requires tinkering – refinement - and more than a little sacrifice. HR-1 moves us in the right direction."

"So limiting gerrymandering would be your priority?" said the President.

"It's a start and the legislation is already on the docket," said Rawlings.

"Makes sense," said Jillings raising his glass to toast concurrence.

"And voting rights? HR-2?" said the President.

"It makes it easier to vote and harder to challenge a voter," said Rawlings.

"But shouldn't we verify that every voter is legitimate, Rawlings? What about all those dead people who vote and folks who vote twice? And why not ask a few questions to see if they have a clue about what they're voting for? I'll admit I wasn't well-informed back in Madison. Neither were my buddies at the grange. I'd see a couple commercials, read some tweets, and mark my ballot along party lines ... if I voted at all. I had a farm to run, and I didn't always make time," said the President furrowing his brow.

"You raise several issues," said Rawlings. "There's a need for a valid voter ID, but I wrote HR-2 to limit screening that's intentionally partisan," said Rawlings. "It restricts the games they play - like disqual-ifying a voter because he can't remember the number of his first driver's license. And as to your second question, if we quiz voters, we're back to Jim Crow literacy tests. The Voting Rights Act of 1965 made it harder for whites to block minority registration. I'd rather focus on getting folks to the polls, not blocking them at the polls. Back in the twenties, outfits like the League of Women Voters ran 'Get Out the Vote' campaigns."

"Voting is my kind of America," said Congressman Jillings.

"Back in the 1920s, the emphasis was on encouraging every eligible voter to get to the polls. But the pendulum swung the other way since the turn of the millennium," Rawlings gestured with a half circle of his finger. "Leader Erling Claymore, Speaker Avril Thermadore and his crowd fear the changing demography, so they hatch legislation to suppress the minority vote. HR-2 limits what they're up to. It shortens lines at polling places, adds drop boxes, encourages mail-in ballots and on-line voting. Election day becomes a national holiday so working folks can vote. Every American should want that," said Rawlings.

"But do folks know what they're voting for?" said the President.

"Your Secretary of Education wants more civics classes in schools," said Rawlings.

"I'm for education," said Jillings nodding.

"And Congress?" said the President. "How informed are the repre-sentatives themselves about the piles of legislation up for a vote? I'm told Congress enacts from 200-600 statutes per biennial term – more than 30,000 since 1789. How informed could you be?"

"A fair question, and since you've been so candid, I admit that my colleagues and I don't have a handle on every bill before us. We have to rely on staff and lobbyists. It's a global, ever more technical world, and every piece of legislation impacts some other special interest."

"So what's the answer?" said the President.

"Comes down to priorities," said Rawlings. "The way it is now, fundraising tops the list. But imagine if representatives could spend more time legislating and less defending our seats. Our afternoons are taken up dialing for dollars across the street, but what choice do we have? I like Senator Van Buren's proposal to shorten campaigns and cap spending. The Brits limit electioneering to twenty-five days. Ours can stretch to six hundred. Last election our two parties spent a combined $2.1 billion dollars. The Brits spent $40 million - way less per capita. I've co-sponsored his cap on campaign spending."

"Yet Van Buren's bill is stuck in committee," said the President.

"Perhaps you would help, Mr. President," said Rawlings.

"Leader Claymore differs from your approach," said the President. "He wants to let power keep concentrating until one party has such a super-majority it breaks logjams," said the President.

"Aren't we in the mess we're in because concentrated power is blocking change?" Rawlings raised his eyebrows.

"So you think it's up to the voters to demand change?" said the President. "Except…".

"…except social media shapes public opinion. Congress is brilliant at distracting voters who might want change. We get them worked up, with fake news, for example about voter fraud or ballot theft. Look at Leader Claymore – out telling voters elections get stolen. You don't hear him talking about health care or wealth distribution," said Rawlings. "He and Speaker Thermadore are the maestros of blue smoke and mirrors."

"You haven't answered my questions about voter fraud. Doesn't it matter?" said the President.

"If it happens, but I'm more concerned that a third of eligible voters stay away," said Rawlings. "What does it say about our priorities that in one year 306 bills were introduced to restrict voting rights, and one party introduced 89% of them? Do we really want to purge voters from rolls; reduce the number of polling stations; waive off disability voting; put Secretaries of State in place to decertify a legitimate election?"

"You've still avoided my question," said the President

"Ever been hit by lightening, Mr. President?"

"Course not."

"The MIT study found voter fraud in 0.00006 percent of the votes. In one state it was 0.000004 percent. You're five times more likely to be stuck by lightening," said Rawlings.

"No wonder my constituents don't see the light," said Jillings guffawing at his wit.

Rawlings rolled his eyes at Jillings.

"Now may I be blunt, Senator?" said the President.

"Of course," said Rawlings.

"Do you think you'll get reelected?" said the President. "Your numbers aren't great,"

Jillings looked up.

"I hope to be, of course," said Rawlings, "but my war chest is empty."

"Miley said you were having trouble," said the President, "that you were primaried for supporting Gammon's infrastructure bill, may he rest in peace. But you baffle me."

"How's that?" said Rawlings.

"HR-1 is your baby. But the bill limits your ability to redistrict. You cosponsored HR-2, which makes it harder to challenge your opponent's voters," said the President. "What's with that?"

"I'll admit," said Rawlings, "it's tempting to turn away voters I know oppose me. But it's pyrite because then voters lose confidence in elections and in me. I didn't come to Congress to camp here," said Rawlings. "Gets us back to Franklin's *a Republic if we can keep it.*' There's never been a democracy that has lasted into a third century. Autocracies outmaneuver us. I can live with being a one-termer, but I can't live under authoritarian rule."

The President paused to consider the Senator's words. "Most of the representatives who visit the Oval have reelection in mind."

"I'm sure you're seeing how the Hill eats away at us. The things we came here to do get moved to the back burner. Rationalizations pile up. *Well, maybe I could relax my position on the carbon tax since my big donor asks me to.* A colleague calls it being 'nibbled to death by ducks'."

"Ducks?" Jillings looked baffled.

"Excuses accumulate until before you know it, kids have allergies from foul air, city water pipes still have lead, and a mandated river cleanup gets postponed. Frankly, your Selon nailed it."

"Not *my* Selon, Senator." said the President. "So?"

"… so we fight like banshees to pass bills like HR-1 and HR2," said Rawlings. "Then we come back in a decade and fight for them all over again because special interests return like weeds to erode democracy."

"That's dandy but it doesn't build a war chest, and Leader Claymore says you're being outspent."

"My opponent's commercial has me on a throne with a crown. She calls me 'The King of Deficit Spending' for supporting infrastructure spending. That's nuts, but she bought a ton of airtime," said Rawlings.

"Isn't the Abraham Lincoln Bridge is in her district … isn't that the one in danger?" said the President. "Yet she opposes infrastructure dollars for Kentucky?"

"Because she got an earmark to fix the bridge. Meanwhile this so-called fiscal conservative spends twelve-million bucks to tell her constituents she's the big deficit hawk. I'm under pressure to raise enough to fight her," said Rawlings, "but it takes some nasty promises to bring in that kind of money. Money corrupts campaigns like that," Rawlings snapped his thumb and finger.

"Which brings us full circle to our fragile Republic," said the President. "Gentlemen, I know less about how the Hill works than either of you, but the Selons have a point. If we can't get government moving, we'll lose more than our titles."

Congressman Jillings perked up. "What do they tell you, those Selons? Do they say how long we have?"

"No Congressman Jillings, I never hear from them. But they're watching, and I think we're being tested."

"That so," said Jillings, looking puzzled.

■■■

Exiting the West Wing corridors, Rawlings turned to Jillings, "For a Georgia farmer new to things around here, the President's caught on fast."

"Think so?" said Jillings.

"Chief of Staff Miley confided he's impressed," said Rawlings. "He says the President asks a lot of questions and plays it cool but knows more than he lets on," said Rawling. "He constantly plays devil's advocate as he just did with us. But I believe Butler might support us. The one thing I'm certain of is that Senator Madrid and Speaker Thermadore have a surprise coming if they think they're dealing with a hayseed."

11

DINNER PLANS

"I BELIEVE YOU TAKE yours with ice," said Speaker of the House Avril Thermadore, handing a scotch to Majority Leader Erling Claymore.

"Thanks Thermadore, and may I say …"

"…Yes?"

"… if your gig as Speaker doesn't last, you'll make a terrific waiter," said Claymore.

"A recommendation highly to be valued given your familiarity with every bar in D.C., Claymore," said Thermadore. "And for you, Madrid?"

"I'm good thanks," said Senator Tobias Madrid waving off the drink offer.

The three chatted in Speaker Thermadore's paneled study in his Belle Terre Way home in Potomac, Maryland. On a pedestal by Thermadore's side was a copper bust of Ronald Reagan and to its side, a copy of *The Republican Club*, a favorite painting of the 45th President. In it, artist Andy Thomas created a fictional scene with Donald Trump in the center sharing drinks with White House predecessors including Lincoln, Nixon and Teddy Roosevelt. To the other side of the painting was a sculpture given to President Trump by South Dakota Governor Jefferson Taggart with Trump's face added as a fifth President on Mount Rushmore.

"To business then gentleman," said Thermadore leaning in. "I overheard Miley saying the President favors HR-1 and HR-2. Rawlings must have gotten to him."

"And the parliamentarian ruled to permit reconciliation," said Claymore."

"We need another vote to block them, and I'm thinking it could be Jillings,"said Thermadore.

"You think he's up for grabs? said Senator Madrid. "Didn't Jillings just go with Rawlings to meet the President? Do we know if any commitments came out of the meeting? I thought Jillings and Rawlings were like that," he held up two pressed fingers.

"We don't know what was agreed to. But I can handle Jillings," said Thermadore. "I met with Ken Brownstein of Brownstein & Sheraton."

"You won't find a stronger lobbying firm," said Claymore.

"They did $40 million last year in pharmaceutical and oil support. Anyway, Ken meets with Jillings next week to confirm he can be had," said Thermadore.

"Jillings maybe, but surely you're not suggesting Rawlings would come around," said Senator Madrid.

"Rawlings, that fucking ideologue," said Thermadore. "A Kamikaze who'd commit hari-kari before straying from his far left principles. Forget Rawlings. Jillings on the other hand is such a weathervane anything's possible."

"And the good news," said Thermadore, "is that Jillings is on dime-thin ice in his district and knows it. If Ken can catch him sober – he set the meeting for 8 A.M. – then Jillings might be listening. Ken will offer 'Jillngs for Senate' enough cash for to dominate West Virginia media. That should get the little prick's attention."

"Brownstein & Sheraton pushed my bill to cut excise taxes for Anhew-Buzch," said Claymore. "They're topnotch."

"But do we want all our our eggs in the Jillings basket knowing how unreliable he is?" said Madrid.

"I have a Plan B," said Thermadore, "in case Jillings doesn't go for Ken's offer."

"Like?" said Madrid.

"Like Jillings might be delayed at the Richmond airport and miss the house vote entirely," said Thermadore.

"What makes you think he won't stay in D.C. to wait for the vote?" said Claymore.

"I've had him invited home to Richmond for a party in his honor," said Thermadore.

"Well played, Thermadore. But why would he miss the flight back?" said Madrid.

"Wild Turkey, and there'll be plenty of it at the party with Roxanne there to make sure Jillings gets loaded. That bitch could incapacitate a stone. She and Jillings have a history, you know. I have photos, and her husband's a mean bull. She'll make sure Jillings doesn't make the flight," said Thermadore.

"Nice," said Claymore.

"And if she can't, things happen to drunks," said Thermadore.

"Maybe the less I know, the better," said Senator Madrid.

"Then we're agreed, Madrid? Claymore?" said Thermadore raising his glass. "In that case gentlemen, my little woman has set a fine gumbo dinner."

"Your wife's gumbo is worth the trip. I could eat it for days," said Madrid.

"You've had it before?" said Thermadore. "When?"

"Ah …maybe I just heard about it," said Madrid.

Thermadore looked at Madrid who turned away.

12

MEETING OF THE MINDS

K EN BROWNSTEIN PASSED through the bronze doors of the Dirksen Senate Office Building and down the corridor to Congressman Gillmoe Jillings' reception room. A secretary took his umbrella, then led him to the Congressman's office, personally decorated by his wife with marble cherubs looking adoringly at a portrait of the seal of West Virginia framed in gold.

"Have a seat, Mr. Brownstein. I hope you didn't get drenched," said Jillings.

"Good to meet you," said Brownstein extending his hand.

"I hear nothing but good about Brownstein & Sheraton," said Jillings.

"The firm's come a ways Senator. D.C.'s biggest now."

"So I'm told," said Jillings. "Well tell me how I can help."

"Actually it's about what I can do for you, Congressman. The current fundraising climate is healthy, and Brownstein & Sheraton has powerful clients eager to get behind 'Jillings for Congress'."

"I like the sound of that, indeed I do. What has folks loosening their wallets?"

"A mix of things, but uncertainty about Butler tops the list. Clients don't know where he stands on a bunch of issues. He has no track record obviously, or donors whose rings he has to kiss. But rumor has it he may go with Rawlings on HR-1 and HR-2. The President's slow to show his cards. How'd we end up with a farmer who never ran a campaign?" said Brownstein, intently measuring the congressman's reaction.

"Bizarre," said Jillings, "President by lottery? Really?"

Brownstein relaxed.

"But it's a good thing if concern about Butler has folks shelling out," said Jillings.

"It helps. Combine that with our latest fundraising tactics, and you're staring at opportunity, Congressman Jillings."

"New tactics?" said Jillings.

"Like enhancements in our email blasts. Seniors miss the prechecked boxes that authorize repeat monthly donations; unsubscribe links that when clicked confirm a donation; and *faux* invoices," said Brownstein.

"Come a long way from the days when my staff typed fund-raising letters on a Selectric," said Jillings.

"But let's talk about your campaign, Congressman," said Brownstein. "If my information is correct, 'Jillings for Congress' is seven million short of the thirty you need. We can get you over that hump."

"Nothing would please me more, Ken."

"But my clients have questions."

"Shoot," said Jillings.

"Like I said, they're uncertain about President Butler and his Selons, and especially about HR-1 and HR-2. Which begs the question, do we know for sure the Selons will accept a vote on the legislation? They stuck us with Butler. Do they intend to control Congress every step of the way?"

"You're asking me?" said Jillings. "I know even less about what's up after Rawlings and I met with the President. But Butler thinks they won't interfere. At least not now."

"That weird avatar hasn't been back on TV, so maybe the vote can go off as usual," said Brownstein.

"Your mouth to my good Lord's ears, Ken," said Jillings, bowing his head and closing his eyes.

"Suppose the Selons do leave Congress alone, Jillings. You read the same polls I do. 'Jillings for Congress' needs cash."

"Something to drink, Ken?" said Jillings standing over his bar cart.

"Nine's early, but don't hold off on my account," said Brownstein. "Wouldn't mind a shot of coffee. Black if it's no trouble."

"I like to start the day on the right foot," said Jillings draining a Waterford decanter.

"We can take care of your funding needs, Congressman."

"My predecessor relied on Brownstein & Sheraton," said Jillings, "and I'd welcome your help."

"But ..." said Brownstein.

"But?" said Jillings.

"My donors need to be comfortable about HR-1 and HR-2, and you haven't announced. Word is you might vote with Rawlings. My clients need to be sure you won't," said Brownstein.

"I'd breathe easier knowing my seat was secure. When Rawlings and I met with Butler, I got the feeling the President favors the bills, so I don't think you'll get his veto. He didn't say so, but I watched him nodding when Rawlings outlined the intent of his bills. Butler might lean liberal. I read that the President spends hours reading letters from average citizens – some aren't even donors," said Jillings. "But what do you expect of a Madison farmer named Jeremiah. What a rube. But if you hope to kill the bills, you'll need every vote."

"The will of the people is the bedrock of democracy," said Brownstein winking, "but the right leadership is even more important. We need men like you reelected, Congressman. Give the people too strong a say, and who'll protect them from themselves? Democracy works fine if we keep people out of it."

"Got that right, Ken," said Jillings raising his glass.

"Men like you keep Congress from going off the rails," said Brownstein.

"I'm called a pioneer of the status quo," said Jillings.

"But you have to win, and I will make sure you do," said Brownstein.

"Music to my ears," said Jillings.

"Though democracy isn't cheap," said Brownstein gesturing with his Montblanc. "And I can make up the seven million you're short when you announce against HR-1, HR-2 and HR-11."

Jillings nodded vigorously.

"You appreciate that change doesn't take us forward," said Brownstein. "The change I want is stability for a change – keep things as they are."

Jillings's Administrative Assistant stuck his head in the door, "Congressman, your next appointment is here."

Jillings took a hurried a gulp, then reached for Brownstein's hand. "Well thank you Ken." He put a hand on Brownstein's shoulder, "This meeting was useful. And you did say nine million?"

"Congressman," Brownstein nodded, "I mentioned seven ... but nine is not out of the question. I trust I'll be hearing your announcement?"

■■■

Light years away by one of the four billion stars in the Milky Way Galaxy, atop a hazy band of light, Commander Gregor beamed his delight.

13

Torch Song

AT THE REQUEST of Parliament, Provost Darius and Commander Gregor materialized to provide an update.

"How's the lottery winner progressing?" said Eminence.

Gregor's brow furrowed, "Aren't you monitoring him?"

"We are," said Eminence, "but clouds of magnetized plasma obstruct our surveillance and all those Selon tourists degrade the bandwidth. You just can't count on reliable intergalactic broadband in season anymore."

"I'm happy to oblige, Eminence," said Darius, "and ..."

"... and," Gregor interrupted, "as I predicted, Jeremiah Butler governs with the ineptitude typical of an Earthling."

"As I was saying before Gregor interrupted," said Darius, "Jeremiah Butler is a quick learner who sees how dysfunctional his government is; that his Congress dodges problem-solving at any cost."

"We hoped for improvement," said Eminence, "perhaps in food production ... carbon reduction ... an easing of the floods?"

"Butler's accomplished nothing," said Gregor, "other then to intensify the paralysis in Washington. In one speech he united the entire joint session against him. And as to legislation, Congress remains stalemated."

"Over...?" said Eminence.

"Everything, especially how best to keep citizens from voting," said Gregor.

"You can't blame that on Butler," said Darius. "That's gone on since the battle for woman's suffrage."

"I thought democracy meant that every tribal member had a vote. What am I missing?" said Eminence.

"The founders intended that they could," said Gregor, "but ..."

"And I see citizens in long queues on election days?" Eminence interrupted.

"You mean the archaic ritual that has voters lined up for hours to scratch pencil marks on paper ballots? A process that could be accomplished in minutes by computer. Quaint how humans stick to traditions." said Gregor.

"But you have it right, Eminence," said Darius. "The American constitution empowers every citizen with the vote, a tradition rooting back to 508 B.C. when an Athenian lawyer, Cleisthenes, altered the Greek constitution to wrestle power from the nobles and share it with commoners."

"And every vote has equal weight?" said Eminence.

"Correct, Eminence," said Darius. "Shared power is fundamental to their constitution."

"Yet Commander Gregor says they battle over who gets democracy and who doesn't," said Eminence.

"Let's be real," said Gregor. "Democracy is the fiction leaders use to corral voters like cattle. Leaders spend freely to promote the equality myth, then citizens pledge allegiance and wave flags."

"Characteristically narrow minded of you, Gregor. Myths are ideals that motivate citizens. Hundreds of tribes in the galaxy have useful myths," said Darius, "but I don't hear you demanding we eliminate them."

"You call it 'motivation'. It's brainwashing. Look at the money they spend telling citizens how 'free' they are. They won't make real progress until they admit they're an oligarchy and revamp from there. Instead they demand allegiance to the democracy myth with the ferocity of their religious convictions. Young mammals pledge to the flag before class. Athletes who won't put hand over heart during the National Anthem are asked off the field. Humans remind me of the Bazzelkrites on Alpha 17 who worship rainbows and salute leaders on rain days," said Gregor.

"That Americans haven't achieved a perfect democracy doesn't mean it's not a worthy goal?" said Darius.

"It not a goal when leaders don't take it to heart," said Gregor. "You've mind-scanned Avril Thermador and Tobias Madrid. Are the flags in their offices and the slogans they mouth really about 'freedom'? Do they fervently hope Congress will function democratically? Or is patriotism the branding they use to manipulate?"

"I have seen leaders using myth to control," said Eminence who'd hoped to remain neutral, "and I've wondered. Without the democracy myth, would parents let their young go off to war? The leaders themselves don't go. It was their 31st President, Herbert Hoover, who said, "Older men declare war. But it is the youth that must fight and die.""

"With respect, Eminence, how easily we forget our own time - eons ago - before Selons shed the body. We went to war. We were primitives. But doesn't our evolution suggests humans should have an opportunity to mature? And while war is abhorrent, doesn't it also show human nobility - that they will sacrifice for a cause they hold dearer than life itself?" said Darius.

"Are you that gullible?" said Gregor. "Patriotism is how elites convince citizens how good they have it - to hide the inequality. Leaders rely on repetition to convince citizens they enjoy the finest healthcare, greatest longevity, superior schooling, and have the strongest military," said Gregor. "They don't care it isn't true."

"But if tribal leaders are so shrewd, why risk telling citizens that they have the same rights as their leaders?" said Eminence.

"Because when citizens believe such nonsense it's easier for leaders to hide that they distribute wealth hierarchically," said Gregor.

"How do you come up with these distortions, Gregor?" said Darius. "The tribe Jeremiah Butler heads is famous as the land of opportunity. Any citizen can aspire to the highest office and leaders have come from humble beginnings. The tribe's reputation for welcoming the least among Earth's peoples is well known."

"A reputation with little footing in reality," said Gregor. "I'll grant there was altruism in the early days of the Republic. Their reputation for generosity was so well heralded that in 1886 the French made a flamboyant gesture. In Paris they packed 350 pieces of a 305-foot salute in 217 wooden crates which they shipped and reassembled in New York."

"I've seen it," said Eminence. "It bears a flattering inscription celebrating that the tribe welcomed *'huddled masses yearning to breath free'*, and accepted Earth's *'homeless and tempest tossed'*."

"But with humans, good intent is never deeper than their epidermis," said Gregor.

"You can't dispute that the tribe took in immigrants from all parts," said Darius.

"I can and I do," said Gregor. "Immigration was all the rage when they needed cheap labor, but when they didn't, they slammed the gates," said Gregor.

"Says who?" said Darius.

"Says their history," said Gregor. "You've gone though our archives. First came the Irish in the mid 1800s – accounting for about a third of the newcomers. In the late 1800s, a second band of refugees landed - Italians and Jews from Europe. That's when the roller-coaster really took off: periods of tribal welcoming, then times of violent exclusion. A rash of laws blocked the 'yearning, huddled masses'.

"Gregor picks at history, Eminence," said Darius. "Selon archives clearly document that the new world welcomed thousands."

"Welcomed? Did you really say 'welcomed'? You found that in the *Alice in Wonderland* archives. Did it mention the Naturalization Act of 1790 which permitted only *white* 'huddle masses' – i.e., Europeans. Or the Chinese Exclusion Act of 1882 which lit off years of anti-Asian bias. In the 1900s they forced Japan to restrict emigration. San Francisco schools separated Japanese from Anglo students," said Gregor. "Landlords hung signs: '*No Blacks or Jews Need Apply.*' Did I add the 2017 Muslim Immigration ban or how they lied about political asylum at the Southern borders?"

"I didn't say they were perfect," said Darius. "Selon history has a blemish or two."

"Blemish or *two*? You want more? The Immigration Act of 1942 set quotas by nationality to exclude Asians. How about the American Immigration Act of 1917 which welcomed the planet's '*tired and hungry*' - if they could prove literacy. Did I mention the 66,000 Americans of Japanese origin that Roosevelt yanked out of their homes and locked in internment camps through Executive Order 9066?"

"It was 1942, and his tribe was at war," said Darius.

"The fact is, Eminence, that they routinely slam the gates," said Gregor.

"Surely they welcome immigrants with special skills?" said Eminence.

"You'd expect that if they were rational," said Gregor, "but we're taking homo sapiens. A foreign-born student who graduates with a much-needed degree, say in Earth medicine or artificial intelligence ..."

"... gets to stay, of course?" said Eminence.

"...is asked to leave as soon as the diploma is handed out," said Gregor.

"That's odd," said Eminence.

"It's a tribe formed of many races," said Darius. "Why do you think they call it the 'melting pot'?"

"Comet dust," said Gregor. "Differences alienate. Bias drives them. White skins segregate from blacks. Swedes hate Norwegians. Those wearing the cross disparage those that show the Star of David. Heterosexuals bash homosexuals. As galactic species go, humans represent the pinnacle of intolerance," said Gregor.

"For a Selon who considers himself so tolerant, Gregor, your examples are nothing but bias," said Darius. "Eminence, I'm going to show you Earthlings that care for others regardless of how they differ. Humans who dive into freezing waters to save a flailing child; go hungry so their animals will eat; provide their own organs to save another. We'd oversee a better galaxy if more species had the human capacity to love."

"And every day is Valentine's Day," said Gregor.

"Notice that Gregor never mentions that Butler's tribe has over 1.4 million registered charities that do every imaginable kindness," said Darius.

"Doesn't that suggest their government has failed if they need so many?" said Eminence.

"Exactly," said Gregor, "it shines a light on an inept government that doesn't provide for its citizens. And having that many charities points to another human flaw: their hopeless inability to organize. What does having 1.4 million charities say about their efficiency? They've formed a patchwork of confusing services that result in turf wars. Instead of thinking of ways to be sure the needs of the populace get met, the powerful start random charities in their own names to boost their reputation."

"How'd you come up with that one, Gregor?" said Darius.

"Are plaques hung on hospital wings for directions? Or to aggrandize some rich donor? They slap brass plates on benches if you can imagine. Since you think you know humans so well, Darius, tell me what percent give anonymously?"

"I'd have to check," said Darius.

"2.3 percent," said Gregor.

"Does it matter if a little narcissism gets charity in the hands of those who need it?" said Eminence.

"My point," said Gregor, "is that humans aren't natively charitable. Greed drives them, and they're selfish and territorial. Why else would a one percent elite hoard twenty-seven percent of the wealth. Or, consider their ferocity during war. Think Hiroshima, Nagasaki. Human nature is best defined by how enthusiastically they hate."

"Or by how passionately they love," said Darius.

"Which brings us back to how they govern," said Eminence. "Gregor, you say that the equality they boast about – 'democracy' – is pure fiction."

"Total myth," said Gregor.

"Then I hope the Overseers didn't underestimate the task we gave Jeremiah Butler," said Eminence. "From what you say, Gregor, the task would be difficult even for a Selon. On the other hand, I don't dismiss that you think Jeremiah Butler will make progress, Darius."

"Jeremiah Butler will prove Gregor wrong," said Darius.

"And archaeologists will discover that the Utahraptor - the twenty-four-foot long dinosaur that was Earth's largest creature - sprang from cotton candy," said Gregor.

"Your case is persuasive, Gregor," said Eminence. "I believe it's prudent to review your Eradication Plan. There's no downside to thoroughly vetting your proposal so that if your assessment proves correct, you'll be authorized to implement it and preferably sooner rather than later."

Gregor began to glow.

14

MOIST SNUFF

"RAWLINGS GOT TO Butler," said Speaker Avril Thermadore. "Without Butler's veto we're dead in the water unless Jillings tips the scales, and we're on thin ice if he's our last hope."

"I thought Ken Brownstein got to Jillings," said Senator Tobias Madrid.

"He did and it was early morning so Jillings was coherent. Jillings promised that with Ken greasing the wheels, he would announce his opposition to the bills. But I'm not willing to bet my seat on Jillings," said Thermadore. "Would you, Madrid?"

"Not much else we can do, Thermadore. The vote's a week away," said Madrid.

"Lose my election because of Rawlings' bullshit legislation: proportional representation; term limits, really?" said Thermadore. "D.C.'s home now. The Capital Grille, the Kennedy Center ... and did I mention my new Chief of Staff?"

"You lucked out with that one - legs up to her neck. Though I didn't hear you mention humidity or beltway traffic in your list of capital delights?" said Madrid.

"The commute gets worse every year, but I'll take the beltway over the empty streets of Carthage. The only traffic jam I ever saw in Carthage, Missouri was when a milk truck overturned. I can't go back and live in that berg," said Thermadore.

"What makes you think you'll have a choice if we can't get the bills killed?" said Madrid.

"Like I said at dinner, if Jillings doesn't come through, who knows what might happen to Butler," said Thermadore. "If he's out of the way, the VP will veto them."

"Come on, Thermadore. Nothing is going to happen to the President of the United States."

"You mean like Lincoln, Garfield, McKinley and Kennedy?" said Thermadore.

"Lower your voice," said Madrid in a whisper. "Butler's totally protected. You gonna' walk into the Oval with a 44 Magnum? Get quotes from a moving company, 'cause Carthage - here you come if that's the best you've got. Or, try a Hail Mary on some Dem willing to swap a boatload of earmarks to change the vote. Did you ask Durbinwood? He'd drive over his mother for an oil subsidy."

"Too late," said Thermadore, "he already committed on TV."

"Then unless you have an idea that's not completely nuts, we're fresh out of options," said Madrid.

"I have one."

Madrid lifted his eyebrows.

"You ever buy from D.C. Tobacco on Q Street?" said Thermadore.

"Yeah, the shop's been there since my first term," said Madrid.

"What you don't know is that the owner is scared shitless of me. I know a few things about his business from a friend I placed at Internal Revenue."

"So?"

"Guess where the White House orders Butler's chewing tobacco."

"So?"

"How much do you know about sarin ..."

"Are you fucking kidding me," Madrid put hands to his ears. "Not another word, Thermadore. Not interested."

"It's doable," said Thermadore.

"Not another word."

"Can be done."

"Look Thermadore," Madrid's voice dropped to a whisper. "Suppose you got it done. You'd experience scrutiny like even you have never known. They'd trace his chaw to the store and be all over you right after the owner caves. You lost your grip, Thermadore."

"It's odorless. Tasteless. And when they discover it in his chewing tobacco ... who do you think they'll suspect?"

"The Kremlin," said Madrid, "at first."

"Yes, and Butler has a meeting with the Russian ambassador next month. Once they identify it's sarin, which they will, he's the first person they'll go after," said Thermadore.

"This is nuts," said Madrid scoping the room for security cams.

"I'm not going out without a fight, Madrid. If it comes to getting re-elected or letting a fucking black-ass hillbilly win, it's a no-brainer," said Thermadore. "He has no right to the Oval in the first place."

"You're nuts to even think about it. I'm sure you ran this by Claymore, and I can guess what he said."

"Nope, I've told no one but you. The fewer who know, the better," said Thermadore.

"And what if by blaming the Russians, your little gig starts a war?"

"Won't happen. The secret service will have their suspicions, but there'd be no proof the Russians did it."

"Besides this cockamamie scheme Thermadore, aren't you forgetting something?"

"Like?"

"The Selons."

"I don't think so. I asked Butler what they're doing, and he says they're staying out of things. After that TV warning and they forced Butler on us - nothing from them. The President thinks we're on our own," said Thermadore.

"But there must be another way to deal with Butler ...," said Madrid.

"And that would be ...?"

###

Light years away, Gregor turned to Darius. "Speaker Thermadore just made my point. Earthlings are a despicable life form."

"I won't let the Speaker harm the President," said Darius. "Parliament won't let our test fail because we let Thermadore kill Butler."

"You can't intervene, Darius. Parliament made clear that once a new leader was in place, humans are to be left to their own devices. They either dig themselves out of the pit, or prove what I've said about them," said Gregor.

"Parliament can't expect me to stand by and watch," said Darius.

"They can and you will not interfere. Humans will be humans," said Gregor, "and they'll prove me right all along."

15

DIVINE INTERVENTION

THE PLASMA CLOUDS that blanketed Earth dissipated allowing Gregor to resume his watch. From a point light years away, he scanned the Dirksen Senate Office for Speaker Avril Thermadore.

He found the Speaker's aides gathered with their ears pressed to his office door which was locked - unusual unless the Speaker and his shapely new Chief of Staff were having another closed-door session. But it was early for that, and the hallway lacked the tell-tail scent of her *Poivre Caron*. An aide checked and found her in her own office, hunting for her laptop's on-off switch.

Adept as Selons are at tuning in to human thought, Gregor easily learned what was on the Speaker's mind.

Activating his VPN to cloak his google search, Thermadore looked for specifics on sarin, especially dosage instructions.

"Odorless and tasteless," he read, *"sarin is twenty-six times more deadly than cyanide. It is in fact the most toxic nerve agent known to man, and the preferred poison of Russian assassins."*

He took notes, calculating that a single milliliter from an eyedropper was enough. Thermadore tugged on thick, rubber gloves, pulled down a mask and over it a clear plastic shield. He held the open tin of Red Man tobacco like a newborn, knowing if a particle brushed his skin or if he breathed fumes, it would be fatal.

Gregor followed Thermadore's thoughts with increasing delight.

But what's the best way to get the tin to Jeremiah Butler? I could use my leverage over the tobacco shop owner and have him swap tins with one from the President's personal reserve. But that means exposing my plan to a third person. Not smart. What about distracting Butler and swapping tins at our meeting in the Oval? His Red Man is always on the table. I like that better. Keeps the owner out of the loop when the authorities decide that half of Washington is their person of interest. But it leaves my fingerprints on the tin.

Looking up from his notes, the Speaker imagined the President after he'd taken a fresh dip of Red Man. Butler's pupils would start to contract and his vision would blur. Mucus would drip from his nose. He'd feel tight in his chest. Finally, there'd be brain fog before the labor of breathing would exhaust him and he'd collapse.

But the risk. How exposed am I? Thermadore debated. *The Russian Ambassador's visit is on the President's Public Daily Schedule, and the Secret Service would surely make him their person of interest before they'd focus on anyone else. There are no guarantees of course ... except one: If HR-1 and HR-2 pass, I lose my seat.*

■■■

Though considered a man of faith by no one, it was important to Avril Thermadore to appear pious, and he attended Sunday mass religiously. A Catholic, still Thermadore chose not to worship at the Basilica of the National Shrine of the Immaculate Conception, preferring instead the Protestant Episcopal venue given its reputation as the church of choice for celebrities and leaders of state. Traveling slowly up Wisconsin Avenue and waving from his limo, Thermadore would feign surprise on bumping into press as he pulled up to Washington National Cathedral. On a good day a CNB crew might film him and save the cost of a paid TV spot.

Thermadore passed along the massive, neo-gothic walls of the National Cathedral Church of Saint Peter - its official name, moving under the 30-story tower with grotesques and gargoyles installed to protect the church from dark forces. The sixth largest church in the world took eighty-three years to build, so magnificent that even a congressman might feel something grander than himself.

Normally quick to dismiss spirituality as peasant sentiment, when the organ's ten-thousand-six-hundred-fifty pipes spiraled to a thunder, Thermadore had the unfamiliar sense of falling out-of-body. He steadied himself against the back of the bench ahead of him. The sensation of feeling light-headed strengthened as the music carried his eyes upward towards dazzling rows of stained-glass windows. Or had it intensified as his eyes fell on either of the cathedral's two oddities: the piece of lunar rock on the South Side's Space Window, or the Darth Vader sculpture. Whatever its origin, something larger than himself penetrated the man known for calculated control, and Thermadore let his eyes close.

The high didn't last, and his thoughts returned from the sublime to the political. He grew agitated, drumming his fingers against the pew ahead as he knelt with his wife.

What if they didn't accuse the Russian Ambassador, or what if the Ambassador had to miss the meeting? Investigators would pivot to anyone on the President's meeting logs. What else hadn't he thought of? It'd been a mistake telling Tobias Madrid that something could happen to Butler ... a loose string he'd handle later.

The organ boomed, *"Holy, Holy, Holy,"* reminding Thermadore of the venue.

Getting Butler out of the way would be a mortal sin – nothing unusual for a congressman, but would he be a suspect? Was killing the president worth the risk – setting aside the penalty of eternal damnation?

Unaccustomed to prayer, still Thermadore bowed his head to ask for guidance ... a sign to help him decide.

The Presiding Bishop took a high position on the massive white stone Canterbury Pulpit, and read from Matthew 13:42, quoting Jesus:

> *"And shall cast them into a furnace of fire: there shall be wailing and gnashing of teeth." HELL IS FOREVER! All who enter hell — abandon all hope! The horror of hell — for even one second is unbearable — but FOREVER!*

Thermadore trembled.

Too big a chance to take. There had to be a safer way to kill the bills. And what about Madrid and Claymore? They'll lose their seats too. How come those pricks weren't getting blood on their hands?

Back in his Dirksen Building office Monday morning, Thermadore emptied the tin of Red Man down the toilet.

...

Watching Thermadore from his position above a flickering chain of stars, Gregor was furious. Avril Thermadore had been a horrendous waste of time. Butler's murder would have been proof positive to Parliament that homo sapiens were flawed beyond redemption.

16

ONCE UPON A TIME

MEETING IN THE moonlit chamber of the Galaxy archives, Eminence drifted to another position to avoid star glare.

"I'm baffled, Seer," said Eminence.

"What confuses you," said Seer who'd been boning up on homo sapiens history since the lottery.

"Irrationality doesn't trouble them," said Eminence, sending forth beams of puzzlement.

"But we knew that," said Seer.

"Yet for a species that calls itself advanced, the way they approach science and religion is primitive compared to even their least enlightened galactic neighbors," said Eminence. "Don't they see how often one thing they believe conflicts with another?"

"Maybe this will help," said Seer. "Recall their twentieth century artist Jackson Pollock because I find his art a helpful metaphor. Have a look," holographic displays of *Mural* and *Number 8* materialized midair before Eminence.

"They call his art 'Abstract Expressionism', but it's a perfect representation of human thought – the way the species randomly splatters religion and science against the wall."

"Pollock says everything and nothing simultaneously," said Eminence.

"Exactly," said Seer, "and when their rudimentary physics can't explain some physical phenomenon, someone with glazed eyes puts fingers to forehead and comes up with a religious explanation. Take creation, still a mystery to them. Lacking a cosmological hypothesis that fits their science, they turn to storytelling."

"They must see there's a difference?" said Eminence.

"They do not. The species relies on 'once-upon-a-times' anytime physics falls short. It's been so since recorded history," Seer flashed a kaleidoscope of human history assembled from his archives. "Take the *Shu Ching*, the ancient Chinese book of historical and scientific documents. It explains that a solar eclipse happens because a large dragon eats the sun. Story has it that the Emperor Qin Shi Huang asked his royal astronomers to predict the next occurrence so his people could come with bows and arrows to kill the dragon. His two astronomers got drunk, forgot to alert the people, so the angry emperor had his experts beheaded."

"Almost charming if it wasn't so preposterous," said Eminence. "But you'd expect something primitive if you go back to Earth's third millennium B.C. How about more recent times?"

"In the early 16th century," said Seer materializing a picture of the *Niña*, "Spanish explorer Christopher Columbus landed in Jamaica short on supplies. The natives fed his crew until a dispute arose and they cut him off. Knowing from his almanac when the next eclipse would come, Columbus warned he would turn the great moon bloody red. The eclipse occurred on schedule, and the frighted natives resumed feeding his crew."

"So they believe a story like it's the gospel truth. But does a scientific hypotheses and a religious belief carry equal weight with them?" said Eminence.

"Not really," said Seer, beaming with amusement, "often stories carry greater weight than science. If a story substitutes for scientific inquiry, they can take it or leave it. But if the story offers a religious explanation, they must accept it. They call that 'taking it on faith', and to accept on faith is considered pious."

"They must be awfully pious," said Eminence.

"Our galaxo-sociologists found four thousand three hundred religions active on Earth today," said Seer.

"They need that many to fill in the gaps in their physics," said Eminence.

"Take misfortunes. Since recoded history humans explain them as an act of some god."

Why did the tribe lose the battle?
Why are our crops failing?
Why did my child die?
Clearly, I've offended a God.

"A simple way to handle complexities," said Eminence. "But I believe they have fewer gods now?"

"That requires a bit more history," said Seer.

"My next meeting isn't for some time," said Eminence.

"Very well then," said Seer. "Around the time man tried to walk erect, a couple hundred thousand years ago, Neanderthals needing answers began pumping out deities. It was comforting to have gods to plead to – the way a child seeks its parents.

"Deities came in bunches: gods for war, love, harvest, you name it. The Greeks had twelve of them in a pecking order as hierarchical as any human tribe. The King-God, Zeus, was deemed so powerful his moods caused changes in the weather. They had a god of the sea, and gods for the harvest and wine making," said Seer.

"Ah, wine," said Eminence sending currents of wistfulness, "one of the few benefits of having a body that I've missed since the Great Uploading. But please, Seer, I didn't mean to interrupt."

"The Romans rebranded the Greek gods. Then, not to be out-deified, Christians introduced ten thousand patron saints, one for about everything. There's a patron saint for beggars, artists, aviators, butchers, merchants, even comedians."

"Homo sapiens have humor?" said Eminence.

"Of a sort. They find misfortune hilarious – a slip on a banana peel or a pie in the face sends them roaring. When the educated began to see themselves as more sophisticated – they abandoned slapstick in favor of ridiculing politicians. Sexual innuendo gets them thigh-slapping also," said Seer.

"Sex is laughable?" said Eminence.

"Not so much for procreation," said Seer, "but sex for pleasure is a comedian's goldmine. Since human prudery and arousal often clash, they call that humor 'dirty jokes'. Their culture still reflects a Puritan influence."

"I find no prigs on their cable TV," said Eminence.

"Because they're more comfortable with sex now - especially the young who have sex ever earlier. After homo sapines learn to read, they try sexual positions from a manual, the *Kama Sutra*, one of the few textbooks college students study diligently. Of course it all began with sex from behind, a preference as old as intercourse itself. Ancient Rome called it *coitus more ferarum* which in Latin translates to sex in the manner of a wild beast. Indian text called it the 'cow position' but today's humans call it 'doggystyle'," said Seer.

"I thought humans considered themselves grander than their animals," said Eminence.

"They used to be told that to be more noble than their animals they had to be chaste and faithful or face damnation. But today sex out of wedlock is fashionable - and they no longer stone women for infidelity … well, least Butler's tribe doesn't. One of Somalia's Islamist groups still does," said Seer.

"That would dampen one's appetite for sex," said Eminence.

"That was then, but Priests rarely preach 'Hellfire and Damnation' anymore," said Seer."

"Which makes me wonder," said Eminence, "if we go back in human history …"

"… wonder what?" said Seer.

"… how their religions spread so quickly when they didn't have the written word, let alone galactic telepathy," said Eminence.

"Cave drawings," said Seer. "They chiseled animal-gods on walls. The Germanics, Slavs and the Finns carved bear deities on totems. Storytelling passed myth from father to sons," said Seer.

"Until the quill replaced the chisel?" said Eminence.

"In the eight millennium B.C., Mesopotamian cuneiform script appeared making it easy for religions to embellish gods with superpowers described in great detail," said Seer.

"That's when they gave up their animal-gods?" said Eminence.

"Humans began to anthropomorphize their deities – give them human-like attributes – for example the petty jealousies you find in Greek and Roman gods."

"Aren't those emotions more typical of a human than a god?" said Eminence.

"They began to consider some humans as god-like, enlightened beings who retained a capacity to show emotions. Take the Buddha. Or Jesus - stories they present in elaborate detail. In the case of Jesus, they tell of a God that sent his only son to Earth to atone for the sins of homo sapiens."

"No small undertaking," said Eminence.

"Then, the story goes, humans kill the son of god who, aided by a Holy Ghost, transforms to spirit and ascends as the third of a trinity-deity," said Seer.

"Some of their gods are both mortal and immortal at the same time. It lets them keep a foot in both places - life and the afterlife - perhaps because humans have trouble dealing with death. They use euphemisms like 'going to a better place' or 'passing'," said Eminence.

"So religions come packaged with an afterlife, especially appealing to parishioners who are frightened by mortality. Religion is their insurance against the void. Earlier, the church sold clay indulgences so humans who sinned could buy 'eternal glory' for a few florins," said Seer.

"So which religion sells best among the four thousand three hundred?"said Eminence.

"Five get best word-of-mouth: Christianity, Islam, Hinduism, Buddhism and Judaism. And as long as you interpret the Christian trinity loosely, monotheism replaced polytheism. Christianity, Judaism and Islam speak of god in the singular. Buddhism transitioned religion to a belief in a universal cosmic force," said Seer.

"Their religions are 'a bag of mix' to use the human expression," said Eminence. "On the one hand they promote the social imperatives Selons value – like civility. They encourage charity, and the virtue of loving each other and urge followers to 'turn the other cheek'," said Eminence.

"Yes but on the other hand, show me a time when humans weren't at war," said Seer. "Their Crusades provided two hundred years of blood-bath with Christians and Muslims killing each other. Both set off with spears to murder infidels and recapture sacred sites. Eight wars brought brutality to frightening heights. Three million homo sapiens slaughtered one another," said Seer.

"I read there was even a Kiddie Crusade in 1212," said Eminence. "Kids, adolescents, women and the elderly followed a young lad, Nicholas, whose god told him to 'go forth and slaughter'."

"I thought their 'heaven' is reached through kindness?" said Eminence.

"Kindness *after* you kill non-believers - to any left alive," said Seer.

Eminence's confusion was obvious. After a pause Eminence asked, "Tell me about their religious adornments? Like the gold cross Butler wears around his neck?"

"More branding. Churches put up icons of Jesus, crosses, and hang paintings of the Virgin Mary - now there's an example of when storytelling replaces science. Jews hang a mezuzah diagonally on the entrance to their home. It's from the Hebrew word for 'doorpost', and holds a parchment with verses from Deuteronomy to remind Jews who enter or leave of their covenant with god. Muslims display the star and crescent on mosques, minarets, and on flags - although nowhere in the Quran is it mentioned," said Seer. "Bottom line is that it comforts followers to concretize the ephemeral in the physical, a throwback to totem days."

"You recall that we too valued physicality," said Eminence, "until the Great Uploading when we did away with bodies. What baggage they were and all that time we wasted caring for them."

"And clothing. Don't forget the fuss about fashion," said Seer.

"How could I. But, Seer, I have one more question abut religions, and it relates to President Butler and your test."

"Please ask," said Seer.

"Clearly Earth's leaders use religions to keep the 'flock' from straying, a term that compares humans to sheep. So why hasn't Butler used his religion to convince his people to care for Earth.

"I'm not following you," said Seer.

"For example, in the book of Leviticus 15:1-7, the Israelites urge men to prune the vineyard and gather its fruits, but then to pause to restore the land. Wouldn't that nudge humans to consider Earth's deteriorating climate? Or is it because church attendance has slowed to a trickle that Butler hasn't used religion?"

"Religions still have influence, Eminence. After skin color, wealth, and gender, religions inflame humans the most," said Seer. "But nowadays it's not so much about this god or that god or different religious dogma. Today man's deeply held beliefs are called 'politics', although men still accept the dogma they're fed with as little thought as they did their religion. Convictions come from TV news preference - the new church of choice."

"Humans always polarize," said Eminence.

"Which is why I wonder if the task we've handed Butler is unreasonable. He faces Earthlings like Thermador, Madrid and others who are, shall we say, so *human*. Is Commander Gregor right?" said Eminence.

"My test will provide the answer," said Seer. "The President needs time. He narrowly escaped being poisoned."

"Though I worry we may be too patient, and with Earth's waters rising, we may lose its Xonium," said Eminence.

17

PEOPLE POWER

"BUTLER," SPEAKER AVRIL Thermadore entered the Oval, seating himself on the couch without invitation.

President Butler nodded, eyebrows raised, "Mr. Speaker."

Speaker Thermadore pursed his lips. "I'll get to the point. Rawlings had the votes yesterday, so HR–1 and HR-2 reach your desk tomorrow. Veto them," the Speaker tapped the table with his forefinger.

The President took a dip of snuff and waited for the juice to curl his tongue. "Then I'll be blunt, Mr. Speaker. Washington has dodged the hard choices long enough. We're masters at kicking the can down the road, and it'll only get worse if I hog-tie the voters with my veto. A veto leaves folks who get past your voting restrictions with even less of a say. You watched the Selon avatar describe the mess we're in. They're looking for progress, and my veto would say, 'business as usual'."

"And what will it say to your Selons when your carbon cap legislation goes down in flames," said the Speaker, "which will happen without my support. Veto those bills, and I'll get your cap passed – just don't be too heavy handed about carbon emissions. I've got coal miners to keep employed."

"I worry about miners, Thermadore, but Congress worries me more. Miley reminds me that you haven't voted for, let alone authored, a single bill addressing global warming, or the rising waters, or the growing cost of severe weather. Seems like saying 'No' is your strong suit."

"Hell, I'm fine and dandy with your global warming thing, but you miss the point. Unless one party fully dominates Congress, we get logjam. Fail to veto those bills and you'll lock in stalemate for years," said Speaker

Thermadore. "Nothing will pass, let alone the appropriations you want so you can wipe-up after your storms."

"Yet when you had a veto-proof majority, the budget for addressing those concerns got smaller," said the President. "The safety net shrank to hanky size."

"Safety net, seriously? The people always want more from the government trough. Their appetite is insatiable. Breeds dependency. They want us to pay mothers to have more kids with fathers who are seldom in the picture. Unemployment spikes, productivity drops, and we get a weaker economy. Do you think that's going to please your Selons?" said Thermadore.

"They're not *my* Selons, Mr. Speaker, and from his side of the isle Senator Rawlings makes the opposite argument. Share power and redistribute wealth and it puts folks back to work. Wages rise, consumers spend more and," said the President pulling his hands wider, "the GNP grows."

"Trickle up never worked, never will," said Thermadore. "It empowers the wrong kind. You get the disorganization that always follows when Democrats take power. Will Rogers had it right: 'I'm not a member of any organized political party – I'm a Democrat.'

"My GOP marches in lock step," said Thermadore, "speaks with one voice, gets things done. Veto those bills or I'm telling you, you'll alienate the only functional members of Congress. Then watch your approvals drop."

"It's not about my poll numbers, and it can't be politics as usual. The Selons have to see progress," said the President. "If they don't, the consequences terrify me way more than ruffling the feathers of a few representatives."

"You haven't been around long enough to know how anemic you'll be if your poll numbers drop further," said Thermadore.

"I hear you, Thermadore, but I'm not running my administration chasing poll numbers."

"Because you never had to win your office," said Thermadore.

"You're not alone in that resentment, but I'm battling for human survival – and that, Mr. Speaker, includes yours."

"Worry about down-the-road issues and by the time they come around, something else has captured the public's attention," said Thermadore. "You'll wind up like corporate leaders who focus on a five-year plan instead of tomorrow's share price. The board bounces them. It's shortsighted to think long-range."

"Did you really just say that?" said the President.

"Use your veto or the Selons will see a Congress that's more dysfunctional than ever," said Speaker Thermadore shaking his forefinger.

The President stood, "Well thanks for your thoughts, Mr. Speaker. I'm glad Miley could fit you in."

"Sir," said Avril Thermadore, exiting the Oval without looking at the President.

●●●

Chief of Staff Miley entered after the Speaker departed. "How'd it go, Sir?"

"Not well, I'm afraid," said the President. "You warned that Speaker Thermadore would get his dander up. But I figure I'll anger half of Congress no matter what I decide. I'll have either Thermadore or Senator Rawlings against me. Rawlings at least gets what we need to do. I'm not vetoing the bills."

"Yes sir, but it might be wise to skip the signing ceremony," said Miley. "The Speaker is powerful."

The President nodded, "Makes sense, Miley."

"A reminder," said the Chief of Staff tapping his watch, "the staff meeting at three. Thermadore calls you a 'closet socialist' in his latest troll, and the press team has a great quip to respond."

"Good," said the President.

"But watch out at the press conference," said Miley. "You know how they work. The same reporters who've been asking why you haven't supported Rawlings' bills will now attack you for backing them. It's what they do."

"Like you said, Miley, it's how they grow audience. Though back in Madison, reporters for the *Morgan County Citizen* were more about facts and less about entertainment. I suppose that's old fashioned," said the President.

"How it used to be. But talking heads who can't sensationalize these days get demoted to do weather. It's not just 'the News' anymore. Every story must be '*Breaking News*,'" said Miley.

18

Two by Two Like Noah

JEREMIAH BUTLER OPENED his family Bible, frayed from generations of use. Often when he felt overwhelmed, he'd flip at random to a page and miraculously hit on a relevant passage. And after moving to Washington, he often felt over his head.

His finger landed on Isaiah 43:2.

> *I will be with you; and when you pass through the rivers, they will not sweep over you. When you walk through the fire, you will not be burned; the flames will not set you ablaze.*

Jeremiah closed his eyes. *I hope so, Lord,* he thought, touching his cross.

The wave of bad news that routinely landed on his desk added to his feelings of inadequacy. A stream of aides kept coming with reports of cities succumbing to the rising seas. New Orleans was one of the earliest to flood followed by parts of coastal Virginia. Lower Manhattan came next, and sections of Boston were underwater. As if the flooding wasn't enough, a quake measuring 9.2 on the Richter scale shook San Francisco.

The President picked up his memo from FEMA.

They're recommending that I evoke the Defense Production Act to ramp up production of emergency supplies. We're vulnerable due to infrastructure shortfalls – sanitation supplies, batteries, mobile communications equipment – while manufacturers drag their heels to inflate prices.

The National Guard's 400,000 soldiers aren't enough to suppress the looting along evacuation routes, and many of the Guard aren't even available domestically. We're shipping trailers from Indiana to the West - and we're short on them too.

Then there's Congress. How the hell did we ever elect those folks? Any layman can see we're in desperate trouble, yet these fools focus on voter suppression, manipulating for power while the empire crumbles. Nero fiddled while 70% of Rome burned – although even that's fake news. They had no fiddles in 64 A.D..

Miley entered the Oval, "They're assembled for you, Sir."

...

Seated with advisors in a sparsely filled situation room, the President turned to Miley, "Does the Army Corps have a new plan since the waters rose faster than projected? Every time I turn on the news, I see houses collapsing into the ocean and families living out of cardboard boxes on roads from the coasts."

Miley pointed to a CNB newscast on a Situation Room monitor.

The President nodded, "Yes, like that."

"Even as our choppers and utility boats pull families off rooftops, we're rolling out a more comprehensive plan. FEMA and the Army Corps will erect portable refugee cities in a hundred locations." Miley called up a map on another monitor and moved his pointer along rows of dots. "And the Federal Housing Finance Agency, that's FHFA, Sir, shut the tap on financing reconstruction along the coasts - an obvious waste of resources."

"The California forest fires? How many mini-communities are we setting up out West for displaced folks?" said the President. "California's vineyards are blackened."

"I'll get you the actual numbers but for perspective, FEMA deployed 140,000 trailer campers to house Katrina victims. We've ordered triple that number - if manufacturers can keep up. Congress is deadlocked over our emergency budget, but as you know we've gone ahead via Executive Order," said Miley.

"Since when is Congress afraid to overspend," said the President.

"Historically the debt ceiling's been raised seventy-nine times, so even Congress ought to know how to do it," said Miley. "I'm meeting again with Speaker Thermadore and his Appropriations Committee. But even if he cooperates, a big if, the measures are Band-Aids. Sir, I'm afraid the time has come to shift our priority to the long-range option."

"Project Noah, Miley," said the President. "How'd your meeting with NASA go? Is General Hooker satisfied things are moving?"

"NASA and Lockheed presented the latest Project Noah plan on Friday," said Miley. "Professor Saji will brief you," Miley nodded to a man at the far end of the table.

Tall, thin, with swept back, black hair, Professor Saji stood, adjusted his tie, and nodded respectfully.

"Professor," the President acknowledged Saji, "truth is, when you first briefed me on Mars colonization, I thought it was another beltway fantasy - a Regan Star Wars bubble. But as I get familiar with the materials you left, I'm persuaded Project Noah should be our highest priority, especially with things deteriorating so quickly."

"Multi-planetary colonization is the best bet for our species to survive," said Miley.

"It is viable Mr. President," said Professor Saji, "but our scientists face obstacles."

"The biggest one?" said the President.

"Man, Sir," said Saji.

The President looked puzzled.

"Specifically, Congress," said Miley. "With climate stress intensifying faster than anyone expected, time is critical. Yet the House blocks funding for Mars exploration and the voyage alone takes 162 days. Your executive order funded the robotic missions and preparatory construction that's underway on the planet. But Thermadore is grandstanding about how he put the brakes on your 'wildly foolhardy' venture. He brands himself Horatio at the Budget Bridge, and his base follows like he's the second coming."

"He may be the last coming, but Thermadore has the publicity advantage since the Noah budget is larger than anything ever proposed," said the President. "I haven't heard him offer any options. Is he waiting for the water to reach his desk?"

"Thermadore's first word as a newborn wasn't 'MaMa'. It was 'NO,'" said Aadhila Jai, Director of the President's National Economic Council.

Although known for sarcasm, she'd observed the meeting quietly until now. "The public needs to be told we can implement Noah in stages; that monies don't have to be spent until each step is accomplished."

"All well and good except Thermadore has Step One tied up in his budget committee, and I'm not sure it would pass even if it reached the floor. Time's a-ticking," said Miley.

"The Speaker doesn't notice that the planet's flooding? His feet don't get wet in the rain?" said Aadhila Jai.

"He's contested each of the Corps' meteorological reports with data from a company his wife's nephew started. The kid's meteorological forecasts tell us not to believe our own eyes. It's loaded with sample-of-one amateur 'experts' and personal opinions from folks without credentials. It insists Corp flood projections are high, and that we're years away from the technology to colonize even if we wanted to – and, they argue, we shouldn't," said Miley.

"When did meteorologists become rocket scientists?" said Aadhila Jai.

"NASA and Lockheed are convinced Noah's viable, right?" said the President.

"Saji?" Miley turned to the professor.

Saji cleared his throat, "Project Noah is immensely challenging, but so far the engineers have overcome each obstacle. It's man's best survival option, and Mars is our logical new home."

"Why, Saji?" said the President. "Why Mars?"

"Admittedly it presents problems. Russian scientists say it's too dangerous; the environment is hostile. Its rust color gives the red planet the appearance of a hot climate, but Mars is anything but. Temperatures can drop to minus 257 degrees Fahrenheit near the poles. It's fifty million miles further from the sun than earth, so it gets less light and heat. The atmosphere's one hundred times thinner than earth so it doesn't hold the sun's warmth. And thin air makes transport by drone difficult. Then there's radiation. 3.8 billion years ago Mars lost the magnetic field that shielded it from radiation."

"Hardly Club Med," said Aadhila Jai.

The President's brow furrowed, "Always the wit, Aadhila Jai. But this is no laughing matter. Saji, any good news? What about the atmosphere?

Remind me how we breathe after the oxygen we carry is gone. In layman's terms please, Professor."

"We have options for air, Sir. The atmosphere is 96% carbon-dioxide, but decades ago Rover proved we could extract oxygen from it. Or, we can convert the brine sea just below the surface to oxygen. The third option is already proving viable," Professor Saji held three fingers up. "Harvesting water and fuel from the Martian soil. Robotic mining is extracting hydrogen and storing it for man's arrival."

"How many will go on the first voyage, Saji?" said the President.

"Depends," said Saji. "The data on how much water and fuel can be stored before the first team arrives isn't finalized. The number of passengers carried, and the supplies stored must match, of course. But the conditions here on Earth are a factor also. The urgency to carry more passengers grows as Earth gets less inhabitable."

The President paused to absorb, then turned to Saji, "What else …?"

"Robotics and three-dimensional printers have started construction preparing for man's arrival – the buildings will shield humans from cosmic radiation and toxic Mars soil," said Saji.

"Heavy radiation too. Good lord Saji, the list of dangers grows," said the President wiping his forehead. "Mars is the only option?"

"We considered Saturn's moons, Enceladus, and Titan and Jupiter's moon Europa because they hint at life. But we don't know enough about them, and we know even less about options beyond our own solar system," said Saji.

"Mars is the best choice in the time we have," said Miley.

"And there are pluses to Mars, Mr. President," said Saji, "features favoring colonization. Mars gravity is about a third of Earth's which makes heavy objects easier to move during construction. And, at a mere two hundred forty-one million miles from earth, galactically speaking Mars is a neighbor. The Mars day is about twenty-four hours, like ours. It has sunlight and an atmosphere with CO_2, Nitrogen and argon. By compressing that atmosphere, we can grow plants.

"Hardly Georgia farmland," said Aadhila Jai.

Professor Saji forced a chuckle. "But we know that lichen and cyano-bacteria adapt and even photosynthesize on Mars. That means food, fuel and oxygen."

"Encouraging," said the President.

"It is, Sir," said Professor Saji.

"And the transport issues, Saji?" said Miley. "The rockets?"

"With your permission, Miley, I think Dr. Cotterswicken can better cover that," said Professor Saji, nodding with closed eyes to the Doctor.

Abraham Cotterswicken, elderly and obese with a watermelon belly, pushed out of his chair, breathing heavily and rising slowly. Yellow finger stains hinted at his favorite vice.

"Mr. President," Cotterswicken gasped for breath. "So … first we boost our StarShips to geosynchronous orbit, a height of 22,236 miles, and they circle earth." Teetering, Dr. Cotterswick flattened a hand on the mahogany conference table for stability. "In orbit we refill tanks with a methane/oxygen propellant. Enough for the 127-million-mile, 162 day voyage to Mars, depending on where Mars is in orbit when we leave."

"And passenger capacity, Dr.?" said Miley.

"It could change, Miley," said Cotterswicken, the roll under his chin wobbling. "The ships already deployed for construction have been smaller. But the plan now is for the passenger StarShip to have a hundred cabins. At two to three souls a cabin, we max out at two hundred fifty colonists a flight. Once the initial StarShip is built and launched, the priority turns to getting more rockets manufactured and launched – think World War II worker mobilization. We'll keep the emigrates coming, but it'll take time and trillions."

The President leaned over and whispered to Miley, "I can hear Thermadore on the talk shows whining about Presidential overreach."

"He'll never support colonization," said Miley, "even when the oceans rise over his ankles. We have to outmaneuver him."

The President turned back to Cotterswicken, "Do we have the rocket technology, Dr.?"

Cotterswicken dropped his pen, flailing to retrieve it. "Yes Sir," It's a multidisciplinary effort with teams from private enterprise cooperating. Lockheed and NASA have the lead."

"Half of Congress will whine that we're out-of-control spenders while the rest elbow for tickets on the first StarShip," said Aadhila Jai.

"Wish we could give priority to those who vote with us," said Miley, "but the courts would scuttle that."

President Butler took a dip of snuff, "Though that raises an issue. How do we select who goes?"

"Gorian?" Miley turned to Gorian Greggorhorm, Project Noah's Director of Cargo and youngest member in the room.

Gorian, the only advisor in a three-piece suit, ready, well-rehearsed and eager, jumped to his feet. "My task force proposes we choose half the passengers by lottery."

"Forgive the irony," said Aadhila Jai.

The President grimaced and leaned into Miley, "Despite Jai's financial credentials, she's annoying me."

"Ah …" Gorian continued, "… we pick the other half for essential skills based on selection criteria I've proposed. The mix of lottery and skills is intended to prevent mobs from fighting for seats since in theory everyone has a chance. But fights will still break out, and there will be scams – false tickets, congressional bribes for seats and more serious crimes to get on board."

Miley held up his palm to interrupt Gorian and turned to the President, "We were going to recommend that you create a new Cabinet-level Secretary to direct selection, but figured we could kiss the planet goodbye by the time any nominee won Senate approval - article II, section 2 and all. Instead, we suggest you name nine professionals by Executive Order. They'll act as judges and follow NASA's selection guidelines."

"…except that unlike the Supreme Court, their choices can not be political," Aadhila Jai interrupted Miley.

"Emigration will be on an emergency basis until the first million settle on Mars," said Dr. Cotterswicken, gripping his chair tightly. "That's a tiny percent of Earth's population, but the four thousand round trips required strain our resources. The rockets can return and be reused, and plans for larger capacity transports are on the drawing boards."

"Okay – so give me the updated budget for all this – but let me sit first," said the President.

"CBC still scores it at $20 trillion, Sir," said Jai.

"Lord, I can see Thermadore leaking it on *Meet the People*," said the President, "and he's already pressing for impeachment."

"We had to brief the Speaker, though on a 'for-your-eyes-only basis,'" said Miley.

"A guarantee that Thermadore will leak it," said Aadhila Jai, elbowing Professor Raji.

The President leaned over to Miley, "I want her gone."

Miley nodded.

"What was Thermadore's response to $20 trillion?" said the President.

"That he'll drown before he'd support such reckless spending."

"Then he'll get the chance," said the President.

"Nothing is more important to Thermadore that looking budget-conscious to his base," said Miley.

"Hope he owns a wet suit," said Aadhila Jai.

Miley faced Aadhila Jai, miming a knife across his throat, then turned to the President, "I'm seeing Thermadore tomorrow, and your press team meets in an hour on how to present Project Noah to the public. To explain it's about survival yet not cause panic."

"A tough tight-rope to walk," said the President. "Once the budget goes public, it'll fire up Thermadore's impeachment effort which is already gaining steam."

■■■

Alone in the Oval, Jeremiah Butler traced the grains of his desk, overwhelmed by the obstacles that kept coming.

I can't do this," he thought. *"Gammon and his predecessors should have addressed climate before the weather got this bad. Bridges buckle swallowing cars, fires blacken fields. And the rain, the endless rain. What am I supposed to do about rain that never quits? I don't know if anyone's capable of dealing with this, but it's obvious to everyone here that I'm over my head. I'm neither experienced nor savvy enough, and Congress resents me though I can't image why anyone wants this job.*

The solutions my Cabinet offer make sense, but Congress won't pass them. What were the Selons thinking, dropping me into this swamp ... a capital that never functioned in the first place, let alone with me in command? I have to resign.

But how can I do that to the people? If I let Thermadore win, no one has a chance. His cronies have no backbone … ostriches. So what do I do?

The president sank his head in his hands, closed his eyes to let the tension ripple, and turned as he often did to prayer.

"Lord, I'm stuck, and people suffer. We may not deserve your grace, but for every Thermadore you've created wonderful, caring people who'd save a stranger as quickly as they'd save themselves. If you have a plan, I beg you to reveal it; to give me the strength to carry it through. Please Jesus, almighty God, help me for I'm floundering."

Jeremiah reached for his family Bible and searched the pages, this time looking specifically for Genesis 18:20. His fingers found and traced the words which he whispered aloud:

> *And the Lord said, because the cry of Sodom and Gomorrah is great, and because their sin is very grievous; I will go down now, and see whether they have done altogether according to the cry of it, which is come unto me; and if not, I will know. And the men turned their faces from thence, and went toward Sodom: but Abraham stood yet before the Lord. And Abraham drew near, and said, Wilt thou also destroy the righteous with the wicked?*

19

Caribbean Holiday

Darius visited Seer on the Eastern quadrant of the Northern sector of the Milky Way Galaxy. He found Seer deep in concentration as was his habit, reviewing the archives that, as Galactic Archival Director, he was charged to maintain - zillions of brontobytes of data chronicling trillions of planets, species, asteroids and comets.

"Hard at study as always, Seer" said Darius.

"Welcome Provost Darius, an unexpected pleasure. It's been eons since you visited my athenaeum," said Seer.

"You appear to be in the middle of something, but might I have a moment," said Darius.

"Always for you Provost Darius. I've been studying the Pretorians of Earendel, surely one of the more unique species in our charge."

"The Pretorians, yes, quite the celestial oddity. If I recall they reproduce unlike any other species. They give birth in a chemistry lab. Lacking sexuality, they arrive together in a great festival to mix chemicals out of which bubble up their offspring. Gives new meaning to the human term 'test-tube baby'. This happens once an eon at their Festival of Repopulation. Do I have it right, Seer?" said Darius.

"Impressive, Provost Darius. You remember them well. But how can I help," said Seer.

"With your wise counsel Seer. You are always objective and know the ways of the Milky Way like few others."

"You flatter me Darius," said Seer.

"I've been questioning how effectively I've advocated for the homo sapiens," said Darius.

"Yes?" said Seer.

"My fear is that Gregor is convincing Eminence and the Overseers that humans are hopeless and shouldn't be spared," said Darius. "I know you are testing them, but I feel Gregor's arguments could predispose their point of view. I don't think I'm holding my own with them."

"I must agree," Darius.

"What do you suggest, Seer?"

"Gregor makes his case against the species more aggressively, while you have been rather passive, Darius, mostly responding defensively. Take a stand. Take the lead ... be forceful. Offer points that make Gregor counter you rather than always trying to dispute what he's said. Show Eminence and the Overseers why the species should remain," said Seer. "Even I'm unsure what about them appeals to you. Make your attraction clear as a crystal so we have no doubt."

"I knew I could come to you for good advice. Thank you, Seer. Your reputation for wise counsel is proven again."

...

Darius entered the Hall of Decision and floated up to Eminence who had Gregor at his side.

"I don't know why you're so down on humans, Gregor, when you're fine with the likes of those dreadful Bazzelkrites," said Darius. "But Eminence, I'm here to prove humans are better than he would have you believe. Humans are compassionate, self-sacrificing."

"Like Stalin, Hitler and Putin," said Gregor.

"I haven't seen a lot of sacrifice from their Congress, Darius," said Eminence, "but I'm open to what you're here to tell us,"

"Actually Eminence, I intend to show rather than tell you. Earthlings have an expression - something like - 'A picture is a thousand words of worth'. So I beg your indulgence," said Darius.

"Of course," said Eminence.

"This will be interesting," said Gregor, "I'm a fan of fiction."

"You will see a side of human nature that's every bit as characteristic as Gregor's biased picture. I've readied The Experience Chamber, and with your permission, we'll teleport back to Earth in the year 2021. We're headed to Haiti, a small island off the East Coast of North America in the time before The Great Flood submerged the Caribbean Island.

"I'm not surprised you had to go so remote to find human decency?" said Gregor.

"Allow him to continue, Gregor," said Eminence.

"Even before the flood, Haiti was beset with quakes, storms, political unrest, illness, and poverty. Earthlings speak of the island as 'cursed'. Yet Haiti had charm: a welcoming people, eye-popping art, and a uniquely Haitian rhythm that permeated the island - a blend of European and African traditions rooted in the French colonization of San Dominque."

"Very interesting and oh so irrelevant," said Gregor. "You waste Eminence's time."

"Gregor!" said Eminence. "Though I do wonder why you're taking us to an island that no longer exists."

"Bear with me Eminence," said Darius.

As if a moist cloud settled, The Experience Chamber materialized over the three Selons and tunneled them back to August in the year 2021. The Chamber reformed over Haiti's colorful Iron Market, the *Marché de Fer* as known locally. Vendors in stalls vied for the attention of shoppers, hawking brightly colored fruits, raw spices and grains filling woven baskets. Though the Great Flood had not yet engulfed the island, global warming had dealt it several blows.

The Selons watched unseen. "That's CNB-TV setting up to report," Darius pointed to a crew arranging cameras.

"Speed." said the cameraman zooming in on Amil Slater's face and rolling as her mic went live.

"From Port-au-Prince, Haiti, Amil Slater reporting. Just weeks ago Hurricane Grace made landfall at the resort town of Tecolutla near here - ripping the island with winds gusting to one-hundred-twenty miles an hour. Nearly fifty inches of rain fell in a twenty-four-hour period, flooding streets and homes before Grace finally weakened to a tropical storm."

The Selons watched Slater's monitor show trees bending and a roof shearing off a house frame.

"Catastrophic as Grace was," Slater continued, "yesterday nature struck Haiti another blow. An earthquake resulting from an oblique-reverse faulting hit near Haiti's Enriquillo-Plantain Garden zone. Viewers may know that a quakes' destructive force is relative to its eruption depth. The shallower that point, the greater its havoc. This quake hit at a depth of a mere 6.2 miles below the surface – very shallow – so damage to the heavily populated community was immense. One hundred thirty-seven thousand buildings were flattened or damaged. Scenes like this were common – the cameraman panned past piles of gray concrete, skeletal home structures and beams protruding from mounds of broken rock.

"Two hundred seventeen thousand children suffered from acute malnutrition and gangs roamed for food. Cholera and COVID pandemics infected some eight hundred nineteen thousand people and claimed nearly ten thousand lives," said Slater as her cameraman showed bodies laid on sheets in streets. With few partially intact homes remaining, Haitian families huddled for shelter during aftershocks." The reporter and crew faded from view.

"Such misery," said Eminence.

"So Earth has storms like other planets," said Gregor. "Is there a point?"

"I want you to see how Haitians dealt with it." Darius scrubbed the time-track ahead a day and The Experience Chamber hovered beside the frame of a battered home with only partial walls remaining. A mother, four children at her side, sheltered under a wet, blue tarp.

"If we're supposed to feel pity," said Gregor, "let me remind you that we're seeing the result of human-induced global warming, and there are disasters like this all over Earth. Human indifference to the planet caused this, and we could have taken your little tour from Seer's video archives. What's the point of dragging us here?"

"Are you ever patient?" said Darius.

"But get to the point," said Eminence.

"Watch please," said Darius.

A stocky man in a green military fatigue approached the rubble and pulled the blue tarp aside. Fearful, the mother jumped between him and her children, pulling them under her protective arm. A child whimpered.

"C'est sur," said the soldier in musical Haitian Creole. "I'm bringing you this," he handed the woman a bowl of white rice. "For you and the children."

The woman eyed the bowl suspiciously.

"Safe, safe. *C'est bon.* It's okay." The soldier swallowed a pinch of rice as the mother watched. *"La nourriture est bonne.* Feed them," he said.

The woman finally took the bowl. Rather than devour the rice herself, or feed her children who stretched for the bowl, the woman took a rusty tin and carefully scraped half of the rice into it."

"What are you doing?" said the soldier raising hands in dismay. "Feed your children."

"No," the woman held up the second tin, "for my neighbor's children," she gestured towards a tarp across the alley. "Her children are hungry too." She handed her own bowl to her eldest child and crossed the alley to her neighbor.

Darius made sure Eminence was attentive, then seeing his point made, the scene dissolved, and The Experience Chamber reformed in present Selon time.

"That's human nature, and it's at least as typical as what Gregor shows you," said Darius.

"Point taken," said Eminence.

"Not so fast, Eminence. What you saw only proves what I've said about humans," said Gregor.

"How can you say that?" said Darius.

"How indeed?" said Eminence.

"It proves that the homo sapiens is among the most irrational creature in the Galaxy," said Gregor. "The soldier gave her enough food to keep a single family alive for a day. And what did she do? She gave half away - assuring that neither she nor her neighbor would survive. That's the mindless human for you."

"Only you could twist kindness that way," said Darius.

"Not only that Eminence, but Darius had to search for a crisis like an earthquake to find a human pushed to selflessness. I've showed you how humans behave routinely - when their lives aren't in jeopardy," said Gregor.

"I see," Eminence pondered. "Darius, have you an example from a situation that isn't a crisis?"

"Benevolence is common," said Darius. "I'll show you."

Darius summoned The Experience Chamber, turning time back to November 2, 2021. The Selons hovered near the finish line at 67th Street in Central Park for the 50th running of the New York City Marathon. "It's an annual event," Darius explained, "to raise money for charities and celebrate sports. The 26.2 mile race is grueling for humans yet it draws thirty-three thousand runners from all over Earth – from renowned marathoners to average citizens. They train for months, and the fastest times determine the winners. Simply completing the course is an accomplishment a runner never forgets. Two hundred compete in wheelchairs. Double amputees run on prosthetic legs. What better example of the 'can-do' spirit of the homo sapiens."

"It's a damn race," said Gregor, "and aggressive earthlings do what it takes to shove and push ahead. I read that some sneak to the subway for part of the race and pretended they ran the distance."

Darius ignored him. "Here's why I brought you Eminence." Darius pointed out a group of runners nearing the finish line. Completely spent, a black American in a bright racer's tank top, stumbled. Nothing left, he sunk to the street and lay prone, unable to complete the race, the finish a mere 200 meters from where he collapsed.

"So, they're clumsy?" said Gregor.

"Watch," said Darius.

Two total strangers nearing the finish passed the fallen runner, paused, then came back. They gently lifted the stranger by his arms, helped him to his feet, and eased him slowly ahead, his legs half-buckling from the struggle to stay erect. A third runner, seeing the others helping, stopped and walked behind the exhausted runner, ready to assist should he fall backwards. The three helped him cross the line and finish the grueling race. The crowd erupted in cheers.

"That's the human spirit," said Darius.

"Such kindness," said Eminence as the Experience Bubble departed.

"Hardly," said Gregor. "It cost the three helpers nothing. The winner was already determined so stopping was no sacrifice. And did you see

95

their faces as they crossed the finish - bloated with moral superiority, thrilled to show that they'd helped a black man. Standard white-skin condescension."

"Your problem Gregor is that you only see the worst in human nature. I'd hate to be in your skin - should Selons ever regain skins," said Darius.

"Nonsense," said Gregor. "Your sentimentality is unworthy of a Selon. Humans are a hateful, emotional, irrational lot, destroying their once hospitable planet. Tell me Eminence, that Darius has finally tried your patience."

Eminence said nothing and neither Gregor nor Darius could read his reaction.

20

OF THE PEOPLE, FOR THE PEOPLE

"Could any American president succeed today?" said Darius. "The tribe routinely ranks Lincoln at the top, but the challenges facing Butler are greater than the civil war. Is what we've asked of him reasonable?"

"He occupies the most powerful office on Earth," said Gregor.

"But his challenges include a Congress that won't acknowledge what's happening to Earth," said Darius. "Speaker Thermadore blocks Butler at every move. He's boxed in."

"Thermadore lusts for revenge because Butler didn't veto HR-1 and HR-2 so the Speaker's reelection is no longer a *fait accompli*," said Gregor. "The Speaker's rage is typical of the anger that blinds the human."

"But he also wants Butler out so he can take his place. Why else is he driving the House to impeach the President? That, and to punish the President for giving voters a greater say," said Darius.

"I thought the framers wanted citizens to have a voice. Isn't that why they took up arms against King George? So the populace made the decisions, not a monarch?" said Eminence.

"They favored majority rule in 1776, but no longer," said Gregor. "Majority rule is a casualty along with bipartisanship when the parties are this alienated. Important bills require a 'supermajority' – for example in the Senate it takes sixty votes, not fifty."

"So in a democracy the majority rules but only once in a while?" said Eminence.

"It's complicated," said Darius.

"Ah, and bless the little Earthlings for inventing the filibuster," said Gregor.

"A vacuum cleaner?" said Eminence.

"Not 'dust-buster'- *'filibuster'.* It comes from a Dutch word appropriately meaning 'pirate'. It's the congressional practice of restricting majority rule to ensure that a single representative can obstruct the whole congress. One legislator can hold the floor for hours and stall a vote," said Gregor.

"It takes a supermajority, two-thirds, to invoke cloture and halt a filibuster. The filibuster insures stalemate and blocks everything Butler tries," said Gregor.

"How long has this been going on?" said Eminence.

"Centuries - since 1837 when supporters filibustered to stop the Whigs from censuring President Andrew Jackson," said Darius.

"Again this makes no sense. First you tell me democracy is rule by a majority. Then it's by a 'supermajority,' and now it's by one person? Then how's it different from the monarchy they overturned?" said Eminence.

"When you have a king or an autocrat, a single leader has dictatorial control," said Gregor. "In Butler's Republic, thanks to the filibuster, although a single member can thwart a vote, usually it's a different person every time. It's how they make sure that nobody's in charge.

"Representatives stall progress by talking for hours," said Gregor. "The record is held by Senator Strom Thurmond from South Carolina who talked for twenty-four hours and eighteen minutes to kill the Civil Rights Act of 1957. Thurmond physically trained for his filibuster taking steam baths to dehydrate, figuring he could hold his urine longer.

"Didn't work, and he would have lost the floor except Senator Barry Goldwater stepped up to save him. Goldwater held the podium while Thurmond headed for the bathroom. Clearly Thurmond's steam bath plan didn't work, so his staff came up with Plan B. They set a bucket at the entrance to the Senate cloakroom off the Senate floor. Thurmond could relive himself while keeping one foot in the Senate chamber, thereby technically not having to yield the floor.

"To stall, Thurmond read the Declaration of Independence aloud, but the Civil Rights Act passed anyway. Others read less elevated texts when they filibustered. Senator Al D'Amato spent his all-day address reading aloud from the District of Columbia phone book. Ted Cruz read from Dr. Seuss's *Green Eggs and Ham.* Senator Marco Rubio quoted *The Godfather.*"

"Rubio's choice wins for most befitting," said Gregor.

"We'll know that's true if Thermadore's impeachment finishes Butler off," said Darius.

21

ON THE BREAKFAST MENU

"WE DON'T HAVE the votes to impeach yet," said Senator Tobias Madrid, "but wait 'til the public finds out how Butler plans to spend their tax dollars. To colonize Mars? $30 trillion? They'll know tomorrow after you're on *Meet the People*, and they'll want his black ass for breakfast."

"Finally I'll have Butler and his fucking Selons by the balls - if they have them. My Chief of Staff heard Selons don't have bodies," said Speaker Avril Thermadore.

"Probably why they've aligned with that empty suit in the White House," said Madrid. "It's hard to believe Butler can't see that his thirty trillion-dollar junket will bankrupt us. After our annual salary increase, wouldn't be much left for warships, bridges and roads."

"His budget won't pass anyway, and he's going down for proposing it. On *Face the Public* tomorrow the first question the host will ask me is if I've heard the rumors about the President's budget. I'll mention his little Mars venture and that it'll cost $30 trillion. Watch Butler drop in the polls like an anvil. And since it shows he's unfit for office, the House will have smooth sailing when I call for impeachment," said Thermadore.

"Isn't it actually $20 trillion?" said Madrid.

"Give or take," said Thermadore.

"Mention that passengers can't bring firearms," said Madrid. "The gun lobby promised a couple million for anti-Noah ads, and I told the oil folks the only energy on Mars will be solar."

"I'll say Butler is promising StarShip passage to campaign contributors," said Thermadore.

"Why not. They never fact check," said Madrid.

"It becomes fact when a couple million viewers hear it on *Meet the People*. It'll rattle enough cages to get Butler's impeachment going, and if my vote count stays firm, they'll find him guilty," said Thermadore.

"Brings meaning to the words *'Free at last,'* Madrid. They should never let the likes of Jeremiah Butler near the Oval let alone occupy it. When you think how much you and I paid for our seats, and it didn't cost that farmer a red cent."

"Makes you wonder what the Selon's were thinking when they let Butler run the show," said Thermadore. "But we'll have the Oval back soon."

"Are the nine impeachment managers top notch?" said Madrid.

"Former prosecutors with sterling conviction rates. Harvard grads … except one," said Thermadore.

"Please tell me there's no truth to the rumor that Jillings got himself put on?" said Madrid.

"Had to," said Thermadore, "though he'll fuck up the minute they stick a mic in his face."

"Jesus. At least keep him out of the loop. The less he knows the better," said Madrid.

"The good news is that I've got Chief Justice Sweindoffer in my pocket. That video of him with his hands in his law clerk's pants did the trick. Suddenly he can't do enough for me. Any evidence we bring will be ruled admissible," said Thermadore.

"If only that were true, Thermadore, but the Chief Justice's role is ceremonial in a presidential impeachment. He has no authority, and any Senator can overrule him. Nice try but your video is useless," said Madrid.

"Maybe, but Butler will be found guilty anyway," said Thermadore. "And even if he isn't, the trial will kneecap him. I've scheduled it for evening prime time so a huge audience will watch my House managers trash him. During breaks in the trial, I've handpicked the talking heads for the TV commentary - snagged them from last night's Oscars. When they're done, Butler's budget will be the butt of jokes. Nothing he proposes ever flies again – least of all his fucking StarShip," said Thermadore.

"I like what I'm hearing," said Madrid. "I'm feeling more confident we'll convict him. Project Noah gets shut down and finally the Oval is yours, Thermadore, as it always should have been."

Thermadore looked up at his portrait of the Warren G. Harding, the 29th President he deeply admired, and a beatific smile spread across his face.

"But you're not walking into a bed of roses," said Madrid. "Though the base expects business as usual, a whole lot of folks want something done about food and floods. You'll have to muzzle them once you're in the Oval."

"Got it covered," said Thermadore. "I'll deal with the whiners in my State of the Union speech. I'll announce an independent commission to study the short term impact of floods, famine and fires. The hearings will be televised, and I'm stacking it with a hell of a celebrity panel - like Super Bowl MVP McTroy, the NBA's Kaminski, and Jameel Ortega, the *Ballon d'Or* soccer recipient. I'll ask the networks to postpone March Madness and give the broadcast top billing. And, Madrid, wait till you hear who else I got..."

"... Okay?" said Madrid.

"None other than Elroy Jefferson Jennings, Country Music's *Entertainer of the Year*," said Thermadore.

"Not bad, Thermadore. But what about the highbrows? A classical pianist or jazz star?" said Madrid.

"I hate that shit," said Thermadore, his pink jowls twisting in a grimace.

"Yeah, but college grads are 37.5 percent of the population," said Madrid.

"Fuck 'em. I'm naming my committee '*Save the Stars & Stripes*'. Housewives love alliteration," said Thermadore.

"Well at least discredit NASA among educated voters. I'm seeing a lot of 'Breaking News' about NASA's technology advances," said Madrid.

"Got it covered, Madrid. It took some scouting, but my Chief of Staff found a Florida scientist who'll testify at the trial - heavy-duty credentials. After the government contract I made sure he won, he's prepared to challenge NASA. Guy puts on a hell of a show – hydro wash theatrical lighting and 3D graphics on charts – all showing why we can't produce oxygen on Mars," said Thermadore.

"I thought Perseverance already created oxygen from the planet's carbon dioxide atmosphere. Five grams – enough for a man to breathe roughly ten minutes?" said Madrid. "It was proof-of-concept only, but NASA said they're scaling it up for the first StarShip's arrival."

"My expert calls that fake news – fiction fabricated by the Climate Action Network. He'll reveal that Perseverance secretly carried that oxygen from Earth … irrefutable proof based on documents that are too classified to show," said Thermadore.

"I hope he plays that card better than Joe McCarthy did. If he isn't convincing, I'm the guy who takes the financial hit," said Madrid. "I went long in the market after you convinced me they'll find Butler guilty."

"He better be good 'cause if Noah survives, coal and oil stocks will plunge. And you know what colonization would do to real estate futures. If interest shifts interplanetary, land prices here will drop. Who'd give a shit about property on Earth? Hell, China might let the Taiwanese keep Taiwan. I won't have my world turned upside down by a farmer and a bunch of thick-lens scientists," said Thermadore. "Which brings me to some exciting impeachment news."

"Oh?"

"NASA Administrator Billingsworth will testify and support a guilty verdict," said Thermadore.

"Impossible," said Madrid. "He's NASA's Chief Scientist.

"He's mine now," said Thermadore. "My IRS guy has proof Billingsworth acted on an insider tip from his son-in-law. When the defense quizzes him on the viability of Mars colonization, he'll shock the chamber and say the technology isn't ready; that Earth would flood and burn before even one StarShip could launch; that we'd be wasting trillions."

"Impressive," said Madrid.

"Immediately after his testimony, my teams hit the networks and brand Butler an incompetent layman who will bankrupt America unless he's found guilty. His conviction will finish Project Noah," Thermadore swatted his hand as if getting rid of a fly. "The Vice President is set to resign, and as third in the line of succession, the Oval is mine," said Thermadore.

"Your Presidency will be incredible, and of course you're looking at your new Vice President," said Madrid.

"Don't we have a meeting at 2:00?" said Thermadore.

.

22

JUST US CHICKENS

"THE THING THAT baffles me about homo sapiens...," said Eminence.

"Yes?..." said Gregor.

"Chickens," said Eminence.

"Chickens?" said Gregor.

"And pigs and cattle … Earth creatures they term 'livestock'," said Eminence.

"Okay?" said Darius.

"So in human taxonomy, homo sapiens classify themselves as animals. Yet they consider themselves grander than other animals, thinking homo sapiens have superior intelligence," said Eminence.

"Yes," said Darius.

"And because they rank chickens and other 'livestock' lower, they assume it's okay to eat them," said Eminence.

"A notch below cannibalism, I suppose, and perhaps as intense a species bias as I've seen in the Galaxy – excepting of course Alpha 17's Bazzelkrites who dine on aging parents," said Gregor.

"But what are you driving at, Eminence?" said Darius again.

"Take female chickens – 'hens'," said Eminence. "They cram three to ten hens in a battery cage with sixty-one square inches of living space a bird. The males don't lay eggs, so humans grind male chicks up and toss them into dumpsters. They trim a hen's beak with a hot blade to limit grain consumption."

"Which says all we need to know about human empathy," said Gregor.

"Wait a minute, some hens get better conditions," said Darius. "Humans pay extra for hens to range free and enjoy the protection of a barn."

"But knowing humans let me guess," said Gregor. "I bet hens are battery-caged because it's cheaper."

"Isn't that what a human calls a 'business decision,'" said Eminence. "Calling something a 'business decision' justifies almost anything. To be 'humane' with chickens – an ironic use of the word – costs more, if marginally. The added cost to free-range a hen is about a penny an egg."

"As I see it, a poultry farmer's cruelty boils down to greed and human arrogance. It sheds light on why humans let one percent of the planet's two million species go extinct every year," said Gregor. "They think the homo sapiens is the only species that matters."

"They consider themselves grander than, say, a pig?" said Eminence.

"They do, Eminence, but, again, where are you going with this?" said Gregor.

"Only to note that their logic escapes me," said Eminence. "Given the intensity of their species-bias, how can they cage so many humans?"

"What are you talking about?" said Darius.

"Prisons. Humans stuffed in battery-cages like hens - two million a year in Butler's tribe," said Eminence.

"And you don't see free-range prisons, Eminence," said Gregor. "Cells have two prisoners, and about a quarter provide thirty-four square feet per inmate. Some get what they call 'solitary confinement' and are locked in an even smaller battery-cage for up to twenty-two hours a day – exiled from the company of others."

"Hold up a minute, Gregor. Solitary confinement is for a few hours, or a day or two at most," said Darius.

"Nope," said Gregor. "The state of Louisiana locked up one prisoner when he was twenty-six and released him at age sixty-nine. They kept him in a solitary cell continuously for forty-three years, and all the while he insisted he was innocent."

"A one-off," said Darius, "and not every country treats prisoners that way. Germany makes sure inmates have sunshine and fresh air and sleep in beds - not a steel slab with thin padding. German inmates wear civilian clothes and corrections officers are trained to think in terms of therapy, not punishment. The recidivism rate in Germany is about half the U.S. rate. Norway, with a low recidivism rate at 20% compares to Butler's tribe where 76.6% of the prisoners are rearrested within five years."

"But don't the Avril Thermadore types in Butler's tribe consider it a high virtue to be hard on crime and to campaign on it," said Eminence. "They argue that punitive imprisonment is efficient; that it's smarter to cage prisoners than waste time transforming character."

"It's why they have under five percent of the world's population yet twenty-five percent of the world's imprisoned," said Gregor.

"Isn't that because locking folks up helps hide the tribe's economic inequality? It disguises how ineptly they socialize," said Eminence.

"No. They're just trying to protect the average citizen from someone who might hurt them," said Darius.

"Then why Darius, when crime dips to historic lows, does the number of humans jailed always increase? And if public safety is their concern, why cage so many who aren't a threat at all? Take drugs. In America more than half of those in federal cages are there for drug offenses – many for taking a drug in one locale that's legal in another. And prisons reflect that odd human skin color preference. The tan ones are jailed at higher rates and held longer," said Gregor.

"But Darius, didn't you say that a democracy depends on an unbiased judicial system. It has to prosecute without bias as to color or wealth and be driven by laws," said Eminence, "and … "

"… 'without bias' is the operative phrase," Gregor interrupted. "In actuality their judicial system is designed to insure bias - at least in Butler's country."

"Utter nonsense," said Darius.

"Is it? It's called the adversarial system with procedures rooted in Anglo-American common law that have little to do with justice. Court is a win-lose contest. The defense triumphs if the verdict is 'not guilty'; the prosecution scores when it's 'guilty'. It's a numbers game and justice has little to do with it. Prosecutors with high lock-up rates move up the ladder. Some even hide evidence to boost conviction rates. It's not justice. It's Texas Hold'em," said Gregor.

"Except that in poker, the betting makes sense. Butler's tribe would rather spend $25,000 to convict than provide a public defender for less. The average prisoner is caged for 2.6 years at a cost of $106,131 a year, per prisoner. The average public defender earns $68,000 and handles hundreds of cases a year. Do the math. Hiring PDs is a bargain, especially when a trial finds the client innocent," said Gregor.

"They try to provide justice. Even the poorest defendant gets a defense attorney - and for free," said Darius.

"What fantasy land did you visit?" said Gregor. "In theory the accused get legal representation, just not in practice."

"Don't the courts provide a defense attorney?" said Eminence.

"They surely do," said Darius. "Eighty-five percent of criminal defendants get a public defender at some time during the conduct of their case," said Darius.

"Then tell Eminence how long they wait for one?" said Gregor "They can languish in jail for months before seeing one - in a system that claims the accused is innocent until proven guilty. What really happens is that they're treated as guilty from the get-go unless they're wealthy, post bail, or have their own attorney."

"But judges assure a fair trial," said Eminence.

"Seriously?" said Gregor. "Butler's judges cage at a rate of 639 per 100,000 citizens. Neighboring Canada cages 104 per 100,000."

"Judges swear an oath to follow the letter of the law," said Darius.

"But in practice judges are politicians in black Halloween costumes so they look judicial. Judges and especially justices have agendas. Why do you think Senators battle so viciously to confirm justices who share their biases?" said Gregor.

"They hold grueling confirmation hearings to insure candidates are of the highest ethical standards," said Eminence.

"Or do they spend days teaching appointees to dodge questions and say nothing to win confirmation. A nominees' testimony is as meaningful as a politician's campaign promise," said Gregor.

"Well they're exemplary citizens," said Eminence, "chosen for their knowledge of the law and an ethical reputation," said Eminence.

"Actually, Eminence, Supreme Court justices are exempt from the rules of ethics that apply to lower court judges. One justices' wife had a law firm that charged her clients big fees for representation in front of her husband who wouldn't recuse himself. And when the Supreme Court Ethics, Recusal, and Transparency Act was put up before the Senate, justices strenuously objected that the legislation was an affront to their dignity," said Gregor.

"So politics can determine how they rule?" said Eminence.

"Why else would nineteen percent of SCOTUS's cases be determined by a 6-3 or a 5-4 majority vote," said Gregor.

"Then inmates aren't treated much better than chickens."

"Maybe that's as it should be," said Gregor. "If you consider which species harms Earth most, hens should get the better deal."

23

TRIAL BY ERROR

MILEY PUT A manila folder on the Resolute desk, stepping back like
he'd placed an IED.

The President eyed the label: '*Impeachment Defense.*'

"It's come to this, huh Miley. Does Thermadore have sixty-six votes?"

"Close," said Miley, "The Whip says he's short, but any one of three
undecideds would put him over."

"Jesus," said Butler, shaking his head.

"And how's this for irony, Mr. President. They're impeaching you
because they call Project Noah a foolhardy waste of trillions. Yet Senator
Levinson, one of the three undecideds, pulled me aside to whisper he
wants seats on the first StarShip."

"Irony, my ass," said the President. "In Georgia we call a heifer a
heifer, and that's soliciting a bribe. Can Justice take him down for it?"

"Be my word against his," said Miley. "Wish I'd recorded it. I asked
point blank if he'd promise a not-guilty vote for a seat. 'Let's just say I'd
be indebted,' he said."

"Cute. So the fate of humanity rests on a spineless wonder like Levinson," said the President. "And Avril Thermadore."

"Thermadore's about power - holding it, growing it and nothing
more," said Miley. "He has no problem ignoring Earth's crisis. But what
puzzles me is why he isn't as terrified about the rising waters. Maybe he
actually believes he walks on water."

"But he's winning the publicity battle. It's so much easier to tear down
than build. And to be tough on ourselves, what have we accomplished?
Other than getting HR-1, HR-2 and HR-11 passed, the Selons can see
the planet's getting worse," said the President.

"They gave you the presidency, not a magic wand," said Miley.

"But as Truman said, 'The buck stops here'," Butler tapped the Resolute desk. I love how the press calls me 'the most powerful man in the world'. Thanks to Speaker Thermadore a GS-1 has more sway," said the President.

"Suppose Thermadore has the votes and the Senate convicts you. Will the Selons intervene?" said Miley. "Look what they did to the lottery holdouts who refused to accept you won."

"I'm not sure I'd score it a 'win', Miley, but I don't hear from the Selons. They're keeping hands off. Not a peep when Thermadore nearly killed HR-1 and HR-2. What perplexes me most is why, with a hundred billion planets in the Milky Way Galaxy, do they pay any attention to us," said the President.

"Or why they don't just run the show and save us?" said Miley.

"They could take Earth in a flash if they wanted to. I wonder if they're studying us. Their avatar seemed to suggest that. Can we save ourselves? Can our democracy survive? Thanks to Thermadore and Madrid, we're more dysfunctional than ever."

"It's a mystery, isn't it Sir," said Miley.

"You know I'm a man of faith, Miley. Like many back in Madison, I'm a Baptist, and I try to make Sunday church. Last Sunday's sermon seemed mystically on point - about the biblical Sodom and Gomorrah. God tells Abraham that if he can find fifty righteous folk, he'll spare the cities."

"I hope he didn't look in Congress," said Miley.

"For sure, but if the Selons determine we're not worth their time, I fear they'll do more than melt a few leaders. We're all in for 'sulfur and fire,'" said the President.

The President pointed to Miley's impeachment folder. "The lawyers. Do they think our defense is persuasive? We've got to win acquittal."

"To save your presidency," said Miley.

"It's not about me, Miley. Lord knows I don't want this job. But if Thermadore succeeds, mankind is gone, and he's bragging he has the votes." The President bit his lip and paused a moment. "When he was here the other day, he eyed the curtains like he was taking measurements.

He's a terrible being but a shrewd arm-twister. So do what it takes to pressure the three uncommitted Senators. Promise Mars passage if you must."

"Has it occurred to you that if Thermadore wins, there is a sad but Pyrrhic justice to it all?" said Miley.

"Meaning?" said the President.

"Thermadore's out to steal your Presidency and say the Senate does convict. The VP resigns and Thermadore succeeds you. His first act after spending millions on an inaugural parade will be to nullify every one of your Executive Orders combating climate change. The floods won't abate, the fires will consume us, and Thermadore will stand at the bow as captain of a sinking ship," said Miley. "Though knowing Thermadore, he'll shove someone overboard to grab a lifeboat seat. He's no Commander Gilmore."

"You mean Congressman Gillmoe Jillings?" said the President.

"Not Gillmoe. I'm referring to Commander Howard W. Gilmore, Sir. Of WWII fame for his valor going down with his ship. His sub, the USS *Growler*, needed to submerge fast to avoid an enemy gunboat heading for them. Gilmore was on deck, but to save his men he ordered the ship to submerge, leaving himself on deck to die. His courage saved his men and his ship."

"Thermadore is no Gilmore," said Jeremiah Butler.

■■■

At 1:00 PM every one of the one hundred and four seats in the Senate Gallery was taken. Speaker Thermadore had pushed to hold the trial in prime time, but the networks favored the NBA finals.

At 1:33 PM, once a problem with the podium mic was solved, the Chief Justice, the Presiding Officer, rose to gavel the trial to order, and the murmur in the Senate chamber quieted. Honoring the long tradition of separation of church and state, the Senate's Chaplain opened with a prayer to Jesus. He urged God and all other attending representatives to ensure an impartial, non-political trial and provide justice to a President who had no right to the office.

The Chief Justice instructed the assembled to face the flag and recite the Pledge of Allegiance. Thankfully attending school said the words loud enough so congressmen could trail a few syllables behind. The Sergeant At Arms warned Senators to keep silent on pain of imprisonment, and to cease cell phone video games, a request that fell on the deaf ears. Some played *Candy Crush* although *Knives Out* did better. A few Senators were engrossed in betting on the playoffs.

The trial began with the familiar '*Here ye, here ye*' followed by Avril Thermadore who took to the podium to address the room's pressing concern: when members could adjourn for dinner. Finally, the lead House Manager presented the articles of impeachment.

Congressman Comenius Biggs approached, slapping pages of his speech on the podium and pausing dramatically to look out at his audience. His voice rose an octave above usual, his delivery a hybrid of sportscaster and parish priest.

"Fellow members of this august body. We are here today to address the grievous injury inflicted on our Republic by Jeremiah Jeremy Butler, 56th President of these United States of America. We could have assembled for his failure to veto HR-1, HR2 and HR-11, given the unconstitutionality of those bills. And though they harm the Republic grievously, it's unclear if their passage rises to the level of a high crime or misdemeanor.

"Instead, we are here because Jeremiah Jeremy Butler recklessly attempted to bankrupt our great nation by fabricating a state of emergency and issuing an Executive Order to fund a voyage - his $40 trillion trip to the planet Mars - if you can imagine such folly. My fellow Americans this is a matter of such foolhardiness as to make patently clear the President is unfit for the office he was never elected to. He was forced on us, and now it rests on this august body to force him right back out.

"As Chairman of House Oversight and Reform Committee, I hold here," Biggs waved papers, "minutes of a recent meeting recommending that the President's Cabinet invoke the constitution's 25th Amendment. The minutes state that Jeremiah Butler is divorced of reality, danger-ously impulsive and unhinged. Without congressional authorization, the President wasted an amount greater than several times the Federal Budget on his ill-advised, unproven StarShip. He intended to load it with innocent civilians and rocket them off to a planet not even on the list of Authorized Congressional Junkets.

Gasps peppered the room.

"The damage to the Republic from his plan, if we permit it, is undeniable. City streets would remain potholed. Bridges would fail. Funding for the health care we consistently oppose would be curtailed, drug prices would drop and medical research halted, diminishing our ability to overpay for equipment like $100 toilet seats. At even greater risk, our military would not receive its traditional fifty-four percent share of federal discretionary spending. In turn, the economy would plummet, and we would default on payments for the national debt. Jeremiah Butler is an amateur in a vital position, unfit for office, and his recklessness constitutes a high crime. The remedy is to find him guilty and strip him of office."

The House Lead Impeachment Manager came after Biggs followed by a string of House Impeachment Managers who provided three days of repetitious testimony.

For the defense, Senator Creedence Rawlings rose to support the President. "My fellow representatives, our great Republic stands at a crossroad. Our disregard for Earth's carbon footprint and for the wellbeing of our fellow citizens brings us here. Oceans spill over land. Food is in short supply and the people starve. Pandemics paralyze and physicians are without remedies. By installing new leadership, the Selons told us that man's very survival depends on spurring government to action. We are given a fresh start and a President determined to save our species. Either he's allowed to respond to Earth's emergency, or inaction dooms us. This trial is proof that some of you resist change at any cost," Rawlings paused to stare at a few in the chamber.

"We fall back like soldiers who cower in the trench rather than advance. We pontificate. We posture. We debate - a tradition that's anchored our inaction since 1790 when the first congressional inquiry investigated Robert Morris' finances. We study, restudy and produce stacks of reports. The average federal employee accounts for the printing of seven-thousand-two-hundred pages. That's per employee, per year. The good news is that most of your portfolios include pulp commodities.

"Our fidelity to inaction has run out the clock. President Butler tried to rise above our bickering. Thanks to this brave Commander in Chief, aided by our most brilliant scientists, we have a final chance – one viable last option - Project Noah. It breaks with congressional tradition by offering a thoughtful plan. For bringing it to us, we should be hoisting President Butler high on our shoulders, not dishonoring him. Yet we waste time with this specious trial of political intent. Applaud a President who takes bold action when most deign to take any. For the survival of our species, acquit President Jeremiah Jerome Butler."

Like an echo, carbon copy arguments followed for days. Senator Rawlings arose again to call the prosecution of Jeremiah Butler 'a charade', a spectacle trial devoid of high crime. "I urge you," said Rawlings, "on behalf of all Americans, to reject these articles of impeachment. Do the right thing for our nation and our species."

House mangers countered urging Senators to find Butler guilty. "History won't be kind to Jeremiah Butler."

Senator Rawlings returned to note that there may be no history if Project Noah doesn't save us.

Hours of questions and answers followed and then closing arguments. Immaculately dressed House Mangers were allowed five minutes each to pose for the cameras and offer strawman rebuttals. Senator Madrid, arms flailing like windshield wipers, warned, "How may bridges will not be restored, how many schools must close, how many airplanes must be grounded if we permit Butler's $40 trillion shopping spree?"

Senator Rawlings corrected Madrid, "Fake News. You know Project Noah scores at $20 trillion."

"Thank you, Senator, Rawlings," said Madrid nodding graciously. "So let us put an end to Butler's $40 trillion folly."

The Chief Justice recognized the Senate Majority Leader who proclaimed it time to vote, and the clerk read the articles of impeachment again, reminding that a two-thirds majority could find Butler guilty. The Deputy Sergeant at Arms read the rules, and the clerk called the roll for the vote.

In a room off the chamber, Speaker Thermadore turned to Congressman Biggs. "I think we've got the black bastard, but it's close. We need sixty-six, but fucking Jillings is wavering again. Miley promised him seats on the StarShip and a publicity shot with him at the control yoke if Butler survives. I reminded Jillings how quickly I can shut off his funds. I'm worried Mr. Weathervane is swinging."

...

Back in the Oval that night, Chief of Staff Miley entered and vigorously shook the President's hand. "Congratulations Sir. Thank God for America."

"The lawyers and you get the credit, Miley. It was close. One vote," said the President.

"Image, the human species may survive because Jillings wants his picture taken," said Miley.

"I'm just prayerful we made it," said the President. He closed his eyes a moment, "Thank you, Jesus."

"Incidentally, Sir, I got a call from the White House Telegraph and Travel Office. Jillings showed up, pushing ahead of a line of press waiting for tickets to accompany the VP on a trip to Aruba.

"Jillings demanded to see William Rapel, Director of the White House Travel office, and on meeting him, demanded his Mars tickets. Director Rapel, having no idea what Jillings was talking about and assuming the congressman had lost it again, set him in a plush chair with the excuse that he needed to consult his staff. 'Would Jillings like a drink in the meanwhile?' he offered. After several Wild Turkeys, Jillings couldn't recall why he'd come and left."

The President shook his head, "Anyway Miley, I want NASA to set a date for the first Mars launch."

24

OF MATERIAL IMPORTANCE

"WE'VE GOT TO stop Butler. NASA set a launch date," said Speaker Avril Thermadore.

"He's the President of the United States, Thermadore. How do you suggest we stop him?" said Senator Madrid.

"Hear me out. I met with NASA Director Billingsworth to ask if there isn't some especially difficult obstacle facing Project Noah – something technical that isn't solved."

"Okay?"

"Billingsworth said that while the present propulsion fuels are fine for smaller payloads like the ISS, the International Space Station, they're not adequate for the massive weight of a StarShip with it's enormous passenger and cargo requirement. StarShip obstacles are way more difficult. The ISS has a crew of seven. With StarShip we're talking two hundred fifty passengers plus crew, plus cargo. Nuclear driven rockets can't be ready in time, but Billingsworth says they've developed a new liquid hydrogen propellant. It's way more powerful, provides highly compressed energy and a lot more thrust," said Thermadore.

"How powerful is 'powerful', and I hope he gave it to you in layman's terms?" said Madrid.

"I took notes," said Thermadore, pulling a small notepad from his suit coat. "He got deep into the weeds; you know the NASA type. Anyway, Billingsworth said," he glanced down to read, "'fuel thrust is numerically measured in a Specific Impulse rating or I_{SP}. Modern rockets using liquid hydrogen oxygen have a propellant I_{SP} of 460s. The new fuel has a metallic hydrogen component and an I_{SP} of 1700s!'" said Thermadore.

"Sounds impressive, I think? So what's the problem?" said Madrid.

"In a word, '*Heat*'." Thermadore continued reading aloud, "'If pure metallic hydrogen is the propellant, the reaction chamber temperature will be 6,000K - too high for conventional rocket engine chambers.'" Thermadore looked up. "Ka-boom," he mimicked an explosion with his hands. "'The four turbopumps at the heart of the engine's design must be fire-tested to confirm they can handle the heat. They have to prove capable of burning at high temperatures for 6,500 seconds even though the actual burn at liftoff is about 600 seconds.' Billingsworth said it's a hell of a challenge."

"They don't have the answer?" said Madrid.

"They're testing one. NASA engineers discovered a new mineral along ocean coasts. It's incredibly heat resistant, and they think a coating will let the rocket chamber walls withstand the high temperature. They'll also pump superchilled liquid hydrogen through the chamber lining for added cooling. If it passes, the Noah StarShip is good to go," said Thermadore.

"We're still discovering new minerals this late in Earth's evolution?" said Madrid.

"I wondered about that too, but Billingsworth said it's not as uncommon as you think," said Thermadore. "AI has accelerated our ability to find or develop them."

"So then what?" said Madrid.

"NASA's mining the new mineral as fast as they can. All very top secret of course since it has military implications. General Hooker wants to use it right now against China while their military is distracted by the floods. But Butler ordered Hooker to stay focused on Project Noah. Anyway, NASA calculations say the new material will solve the heat issue," said Thermadore.

"Which means Project Noah could launch," said Madrid.

"Unless I stop them, and I have a way," said Thermadore.

"Which is...?" said Madrid.

"Director Billingsworth is panicked that I'll expose the video of him with his boyfriend. His wife is suspicious, and he's terrified of her. He thinks he can dilute the new chamber mineral without being discovered - weaken it enough so the chamber explodes when they test. Failure will postpone the launch at least six months, and by then Billingsworth says we'll be past the time when Mars is closest to Earth, and it will be too late," said Thermadore.

"And the flooding should delay them also?" said Madrid.

"Cape Canaveral should flood and D.C., appropriately built on swampland, will go under. That'll end Noah," said Thermadore.

"What about us?" said Madrid.

"No need to worry. I've secured a facility for right-thinking folk at Hoye Crest on Maryland's Backbone Mountain. At 3,360 feet above sea level, our families and my Chief of Staff will be fine."

"I like it, Thermadore," said Madrid. "Noah fails. D.C. floods. Butler's out. His few friends will cut ties when the public screams he wasted $40 trillion."

Madrid stood, circled the couch and with arms out, began to pantomime a waltz.

"What the fuck are you doing?" said Thermadore.

"Practicing my dance steps for the inaugural balls we'll attend," said Madrid.

"Cute, Madrid," said Thermadore, "but my inaugural balls will be my *cojones* if Billingsworth doesn't get the job done."

"I hope being President improves your puns," said Madrid.

25

Prime Directive

"Is it fair to eradicate Earthlings because they discovered Xonium?" said Provost Darius, "It is their planet."

"Need I remind you we're pledged to protect Xonium wherever we find it," said Commander Gregor.

"And we've pledged to obey the Prime Directive," said Darius. "So back off Gregor. The whole purpose of the lottery is to show that given the right conditions, human government might accomplish something. Maybe Washington hasn't achieved much yet, but Butler's making the right moves. Despite enemies, he's ready to colonize. And they discovered Xonium only because they tried to solve the rocket issue. Do away with humans now and you punish them for doing what you hoped they'd do in first place. That's hardly Selonian."

"Then where's the Selonian commitment to protect Xonium?" said Gregor. "We have a job to do, and my team stands ready. Eminence?"

"This is a case of conflicting responsibilities Gregor and Darius," said Eminence. "The Prime Directive tells us not to interfere unless a species poses a galactic threat. At the same time we're pledged to preserve all Xonium."

"There's no conflict," said Gregor. "Humans refusal to listen to their climatologists will bring them to extinction. Have they done anything to stop the temperature from rising? It's up by an average $0.32°$ Fahrenheit per decade since the eighties using their earth calendar. Science never matters to Thermadore's kind."

"The 45th Vice President, Al Gore, warned his fellow Earthlings what was coming," said Eminence.

"Scientists predicted drought and fires out West, and rising sea levels along the coasts. Glaciers melt. Animals die, weather intensifies and destroys habitats while their economy is in havoc. And what do these so-called rational creatures do? Whine that carbon reduction costs too much when even a myopic Earthling should see that floods and storms cost them more. Yet Darius would compound homo sapiens failures with our own inaction? Say the word Eminence, and I'll end the human circus," said Gregor.

"It's the *Prime* Directive for a reason, Gregor. Prime supersedes all others. By Salon law we can't proceed. Until our test renders a final judgment, Gregor must be restrained, Eminence."

"The history of their experiment with democracy suggests the prospects aren't good," said Eminence. "Surely you'll concede that Darius."

"I'll grant that the American Congress is unfamiliar with effective government," said Darius, "and if I bend over backwards to see things Gregor's way, I've rarely seen creatures so short-sighted – not counting those the Commander has already eliminated. I'll even grant how perplexing it is that, facing extinction, humans squabble over power. Should Thermadore capture the Presidency, he'll win an uninhabitable planet."

"Humans think of themselves as superior animals, yet a field mouse has a greater survival instinct," said Gregor. "When danger approaches, the field mouse runs. Humans block the path."

"Let the test finish," said Darius. "Butler's plan gives them a second chance. Aren't you curious?"

'Brilliant. Having seen humans destroy Earth, we should watch them do it to Mars," said Gregor.

"That's exactly why we have to complete our test; to confirm once and for all if they're capable of self preservation," said Darius.

"Flies in face of what I've seen," said Gregor. "Humans will do what humans do. They begin with the best of intentions, battle for power, then destroy what they've built and each other."

"Not always," said Darius.

"Always," said Gregor. "You see it in their personal relationships too. Take human partnering rituals - a perfect metaphor. Humans follow an instinct to partner, and since the Mesopotamians they began to formalize a ritual they call 'marriage'. Marriage among a man and a woman caught on with the Hebrews, Greeks and Romans. It's appeal is that a wedding provides a fine excuse to drink and party late into the night while bankrupting the parents. Recently same-gender couples also began to marry, which caused great consternation among religious traditionalists known as the Christian Right. The latter's vituperative objections to same-gender relationships are hard for Selons to understand, since having shed the body, we know the physical identity is irrelevant. But the human preoccupation with the physical drives their intolerance. Still, humans who partner, no matter the gender, consider it important to fully commit. They take a marriage vow and swear to partner for life – 'in sickness through to health' I think is the expression."

"So?" said Darius.

"That vow's a waste of breath. Relationship troubles invariably come, which is when humans jump ship and divorce. Butler's tribe sheds partners at a rate of one divorce every forty-two seconds – that's 2,046 divorces a day, 14,365 per week and 746,671 a year. They have divorce courts to punish couples for having married – and judges to leave them financially bereft and enraged at themselves for ever having sworn to love someone for longer than a night. Then, because they are oh so human, when they see that marriage doesn't work for them, eighty percent rush to remarry.

"In Butler's tribe, more than forty-two million marry more than once, each time bringing along as baggage the issues they wouldn't face in the previous marriage - until the next marriage goes awry. So, tell me Darius, why would you expect dysfunctionals to cooperate on anything – let alone to save their planet? Allow them to colonize and we delay the inevitable.

"Mars will become a battleground in no time at all. They'll fight over gardens. A few will corner the market on necessities. On earth it was oil. On Mars it could be oxygen. They'll sell air at a premium and create a burgeoning bureaucracy to legitimize their plundering. And where will we Selons be when it happens? Here, having this conversation again.

Meanwhile, with Mars on the brink of collapse, humans will hop off to Venus. The cycle is endless if we don't cut our losses," said Gregor.

"You always go to the bottom of the sludge for examples, Gregor," said Darius. "Butler is giving all he's got for his species. Despite the odds, he's made progress – and I'm not talking only about the bills he passed. He is close to preserving his species by emigration, an impressive feat. He's not an insect to destroy like that," said Darius snapping imaginary fingers, displayed holographically. "Selons put him in the Oval, and he deserves a chance to see Project Noah through."

"I'll consider both arguments," said Eminence."

26

BEST LAID PLANS OF MICE AND MEN

"BILLINGSWORTH," AVRIL THERMADORE hollered into his cell phone.

"Mr. Speaker, yes Sir," said Billingsworth.

"I've heard nothing? When did you intend to let me know the chamber failed?"

"Sorry Mr. Speaker, but the test was delayed until tomorrow afternoon … a technical issue."

"It will fail, right Billingsworth?" said Thermadore.

"Maybe we shouldn't discuss this over the phone, Sir."

"Look Billingsworth …"

"The preparations are in place," said Billingsworth.

"They'd better be, Billingsworth because the press will get more viewers showing the video of you and your aide than covering a fucking rocket blast," said Thermadore.

"As you instructed, the press will be here to cover the test. The story should be on tomorrow night's news," said Billingsworth.

"All right then, Billingsworth. I'll hear from you tomorrow afternoon," said Thermadore.

"And, Sir…" said Billingsworth into an empty phone line.

●●●

"Everything go as planned with Billingsworth?" said Senator Madrid.

"They moved the test to tomorrow, but he assured me the chambers will fail," said Thermadore.

"They'd better because NASA's ready to confirm a launch date. Can you trust Billingstorth? Project Noah's been his baby from the get-go," said Madrid.

"I own the son of a bitch. Tomorrow's nightly news will be all about Project Noah's collapse. Every major paper will carry 'I-told-ya-so' editorials about how they knew Butler would waste trillions on his pie-in-the-sky StarShip. It'll make the shit President Regan took for Star Wars look like the press threw him softballs. Butler's Cabinet will have the excuse it's been waiting for to invoke the 25th," said Thermadore.

"What about his buddy, Secretary Quegmore? Doesn't the entire Cabinet have to affirm the President is incompetent?" said Madrid.

"Nope, just a simple majority, and you know how the leftovers from the Gammon administration feel about Butler. It'll get done," said Thermadore.

"Maybe, but the 25th Amendment's never been invoked," said Madrid.

"You're wrong. It's been invoked three times, but they were voluntary transfers of power for colonoscopies - with the president's approval each time. When Hinckley Jr. shot Reagan the President went under anesthesia. George W. Bush's Cabinet invoked it twice for his two procedures. Trump also had a colonoscopy, but he wouldn't pass the office to Mike Pence. It's never been used to remove a President involuntarily until now," said Thermadore.

"And afterwards? The VP is set to resign?" said Madrid.

"Immediately, and I want to be sworn in as soon as she does - while the opposition to Butler holds. There's a handful of representatives elbowing for seats on StarShip, and I don't want them swayed. They're the same congressmen who most loudly oppose Project Noah, so you know the group," said Thermadore. "My first Executive Order will be to shut Noah down."

...

Thermadore's all-legs Chief of Staff entered his office late the following afternoon.

"Mr. Speaker, I was about to leave to beat beltway traffic, but that call you're expecting from Director Billingsworth? I haven't heard from his office. Need me to stay?" she stretched her chest.

Thermadore's eye shifted to his watch. "Get Billingsworth on the phone. I don't know what the man's problem is."

Minutes later she alerted the Speaker, "He's on three, Avril"

"What the fuck, Billingsworth. You were supposed to call hours ago," said Thermadore.

"I…I," said Billingsworth.

"I…I? I…I what? Did the god damn chamber blow or not? I'm watching CNB and not seeing shit."

"Because, Sir…"

"Because what, damn it Billingsworth?" said Thermadore.

"The chambers held. It's not possible, but they did. I don't how. I diluted the coating like I said. I even reduced the cooling flow. But the chambers withstood the fire-test … easily … so easily it doesn't make sense. I did the calculations myself, and there's no possible way the chamber's heat resistance could be that good."

"You assured me this couldn't happen, Billingsworth," said Thermadore.

"I can only guess that the engineers vastly underestimated the new material's ability to withstand heat. The compound is unlike anything we've ever seen. Even the melting point of hafnium carbide can't compare."

"Then what are you doing about it, Billingsworth? I want Noah shut down," said Thermadore.

"But Mr. Speaker, my scientists saw that the chambers held up. And the press was there like you asked. No matter what I try now, they know StarShip is viable," said Billingstowth.

"Then you are no longer 'viable', you little prick. The press will be all over the video of you and your aide. It'll go viral in time for the evening news," said Thermadore.

"For God's sake Thermadore … I did what I said. My career. My wife. I beg you."

"Fuck you, Billingsworth." said Thermadore.

...

The Milky Way is nicknamed the 'Spiral Galaxy' because if a human could view it from the bottom up or the top down, they'd see a shape like a pinwheel. Had either Eminence or Gregor been aware of Darius hovering atop the spiral of dust and gas – and fortunately neither were – they'd have seen their Provost holding above billions of stars, studying Jeremiah Butler. They might have sensed painful angst but also Darius' satisfaction.

This is not who I am, waves of agitation rippled through Darius. *I violated the Prime Directive - just like Gregor when he blackened the teleprompter during Butler's State of the Union speech. It never bothers him to interfere. He can sweep away an entire species like dust. But look at me. I'm no better than Gregor. I've sunk to his level. But I won't let him eliminate humans unless Seer's test confirms we must.*

Altering the rocket's coating with highly compressed Xonium merely leveled the playing field. It strengthened the chambers beyond NASA's calculations, providing heat resistance that stunned Director Billingsworth. The hot-fire tests could have run at triple the heat of launch and the chamber would have held. I hate what dealing with Gregor forced me to do, but at least Thermadore didn't get to shut the StarShip down. Success or failure is in Jeremiah Butler's hands and not the Speaker of the House.

27

WET LANDS

"ANY CHANCE YOUR Senate Committee on the Budget will free up my proposal anytime soon, Senator Claymore?" said the President.

"Unlikely," said Majority Leader, Senator Erling Claymore.

"Don't you think Congress should have a say on the Mars project? And while your committee has my proposal kidnapped, I haven't seen any recommendations from you on dealing with the urgent matters at hand. The West is scorched while the East floods," said the President.

"It's nothing more than cyclical temperature fluctuations that we've seen since the 16th century, Mr. President. My office sent you records going back to when Galileo invented the air thermometer. So how in God's name would that justify dumping trillions into your StarShip?" said Leader Claymore.

"And you propose...?" said the President.

"... about a thousand better uses for the money. It could build a fleet of nuclear powered Ford-class aircraft carriers. We only have eight hundred thousand full time police in America. Let's hire more and retake our cities," said Claymore. "$40 trillion could lock up a lot of criminals."

"At least get the dollars right, Erling. It's $20 trillion, not the fake news $30 trillion or $40 trillion. I can't image how that rumor got floated," the President eyed Claymore without blinking. "And you may be comfortable calling the flooding of South Beach Miami a 'weather cycle,' but I'm not. And since you brought up cost, if we keep ignoring carbon overload, the OMB projects an annual revenue loss of 7.1 percent of GNP from disaster response costs alone," said the President.

"Like OMB ever gets it right," said Claymore.

"They tell me we're looking at $128 billion in storm damage by the end of the century," the President continued, "… if we make it to the end of the century. It's like my mechanic back in Madison says when I bring her my car, 'Pay me now, or pay me more later.' It's time the Senate became part of the solution."

"Reducing carbon is not how taxpayers want their money spent," said Leader Claymore.

"Yes, and leaders should follow, never lead right? This isn't just about rebuilding a bridge or a runway. The National Climate Task Force calls climate neutrality a 'human survival issue' – and the last time I checked survival is bipartisan. Project Noah gives us a Plan B that needs to get funded."

"We don't agree with your climate premise."

The President glared.

"Tell you what, Mr. President. In the spirit of bipartisan cooperation, I'll raise it again in committee," said the Majority Leader.

"What hope is there that it will ever get out when …,"

"… Pardon my interruption Mr. President, Mr. Speaker," Chief of Staff Miley stepped into the Oval, "but Sir I need your attention on an urgent matter."

"Of course, Miley," the President beckoned him over.

"Of a personal nature, Sir, if I could I have a word," said Miley.

"Personal?" said the President.

"About Madison," said Miley, "your farm."

"Forgive the interruption, Leader Claymore. "Go ahead, Miley, it's fine," said the President.

"We just got word from the White House National Climate Advisor. There's been another reservoir failure."

"There were dozens just yesterday, Miley," said the President.

"But this one's in Georgia: The Hard Labor Creek Regional Reservoir flooded out."

"That's by my farm, Miley," said the President.

"Yes, Sir. The water completely breached, and I'm afraid it's taken your farm. The house, and barns - all of it. They wired photos, and it doesn't look good," Miley handed them to the President. "Debris, broken planks, sunk equipment, and I don't see the silos," said Miley moving his finger across a photo. And that," Miley pointed to a section of the photo, "that massive tree got uprooted and hit the porch."

"Our 100-year-old oak," said the President. "But my team? Is everyone okay?"

"All but your Manager," said Miley. "He tried to save the livestock."

"Is he safe, Miley?" said the President. "He's a dear friend. Tell me he's okay?"

"He's alive Sir, but hospitalized. Got caught in the flood wave, but they assure me he's going to be okay. We'll arrange for you to see him when we get you back to Madison."

"Have someone see if he needs anything, Miley. He's a good man and the father of four little girl."

"There's more, I'm sorry to report," said Miley.

"My harvesters didn't make it," said the President studying the photo. "And it took the old tractor. My great granddaddy bought it, and granddad refurbished it - an Allis-Chalmers row tractor from the thirties. 1936, powered by an inline-four," the President grew wistful. "Damn thing ran on anything – alcohol, kerosene, gas of course. Four forward gears and one reverse," he moved a cupped hand as if shifting, then paused a moment before shaking himself from nostalgia. "Forgive me Claymore, I'll be just a moment."

"Of course, Mr. President," said the Majority Leader.

"I'm sorry to be the messenger," said Miley, "but I'm making arrangements to get you to Madison to tour the damage. With a crew from USACE - that's the Army Corps of Engineers, Sir - to have a look."

"The livestock, Miley?" said the President.

"Gone, they said. So sorry. I'll alert Marine One?"

"Thank you, Miley, but I'm not going anywhere until the Leader and I conclude. We're reviewing Project Noah."

"I'll handle things until you're ready. Sir, Mr. Speaker," Miley left the room.

"Sorry about the farm, Mr. President," said Leader Claymore. "I heard you have quite a spread there in Madison. Thousand acres, I believe? Hell of a loss. My folks were farmers, and I know Labor Creek Regional myself

… fished it a few times. Jesus, she's a big one. A thirteen-hundred acre reservoir - twelve billion gallons - if memory serves. You ought'a let the USACE boys get you there pronto. Too late for the animals, but maybe they can save your harvesters and see what they can do for the reservoir."

"Thanks Erling, but I can't deploy the Corps for that."

"You're the President of the United States, of course you can."

"The National Emoluments Clause? The press would have a field day. Justice would too if I used government staff and equipment that way. Why is my farm more important than the six-hundred or so other farms in Madison? But since Madison County is eighth in Georgia farm production, I will declare it a disaster area."

"You're new to D.C., but the Presidency comes with perks, for Christ's sake. A little help in a crisis is hardly an emolument violation."

"The law's the law, Leader Claymore."

"And tradition's tradition. Around here power comes with perks. President Trump was accused of three-thousand-seven-hundred conflicts of interest, and you didn't see him divest. They say Biden's son ran a fire sale on access to his dad. Nixon's Spiro Agnew took a plea for tax evasion when they caught him with his hand in the trough."

"Doesn't make it right," said the President.

"Makes it routine. Look at White House history. Harding's Secretary of the Interior, Albert Fell, went to prison for Tea Pot Dome bribes. Harding's Attorney General resigned over a bootlegging kickback scheme. Thomas Miller, head of the Office of Alien Property, sold German patents seized after World War I. And you can't check on your farm?"

"Not how my administration runs things," said the President.

"It's common practice, like setting forks to the left and knives to the right," said Leader Claymore.

"Not a precedent I intend to follow," said the President. "When we're finished here, I'll visit my farm without the Corps. So could we get back to Project Noah. I need my budget voted out of your committee. I'd rather not get it done by Executive Order, but I will."

"Go that route, and you won't be happy when your appointments come before me. I'll bring up Noah in committee, but no promise how they will vote," said Claymore.

"I can't wait much longer, Claymore. Take a week, but then I'm acting without Senate approval," said the President.

"You can't fund it that way," said the Leader Claymore.

"I can, and I will. The White House Council assures me there is nothing to prevent me. Presidents direct federal funds all the time."

"I won't patronize you, Sir, even though you are new to how it works around here. The constitution invests one branch and one only with the power of the purse. Congress is the tax and spend authority, not the Executive," said the Leader.

"Senator Rawlings gave me a history lesson too, Claymore, and Presidents have always issued them. George Washington issued eight Executive Orders."

"Not to fund something as big as Noah," said Claymore.

"White House council assures me I have funding authority for emergencies. Jimmy Carter created FEMA by Executive Order and gave it a disaster relief budget of $28 billion for emergency management. George Bush responded by Executive Order when Katrina hit, though he was slow about it. He'd have done so sooner but he was vacationing for twenty-seven days on his twenty-six-hundred acre Prairie Chapel Ranch, and his staff felt they shouldn't disturb him – at least not until Katrina proved catastrophic. Well, the disasters we're facing make Katrina a walk in the park."

"'Forewarned is Forearmed', Mr. President, and I'm warning you," said the Leader. "I'll be ready with legal challenges, and you know how SCOTUS leans these days."

"I do, and the courts may be the final arbitrator, but it'll take months, years maybe, for your challenges to work their way up. By then, please God, humanity will have a colony on Mars and a chance to survive."

28

LIFELINE

"HOMO SAPIENS DON'T live very long, do they," said Eminence.
"Not compared to us of course, but longevity varies by their tribe," said Gregor. "They distribute lifespan by locale, providing health services to some but not others."

"What sets the preference?" said Eminence.

"Wealth, skin tone and zip code determine who gets care. For example, humans in Hong Kong have the highest life expectancy - an average for the female of 87.8 years, 82 for males. Japan, Macau and Switzerland are close behind," said Gregor. "But if you're unfortunate enough to live in the Central African Republic, you'll make only 53.3."

"Humans don't control longevity," said Darius. "Lifespan in Africa is diminished by natural phenomena like HIV/AIDS, Malaria, and COVID."

"Really? Then how is it that 84% of Canadians got fully vaccinated against COVID, while only 17% of Libyans did? And if Butler's tribe claims its medicine is state-of-the-art, explain their comparatively low longevity," said Gregor. "You can't tell me they rank 48th in life expectancy because of Malaria. They also led the world in COVID losses – over a million died," said Gregor.

"How could that happen?" said Eminence.

"Leaders like Speaker Thermadore assured followers that COVID, if it was even real, was no more dangerous than the common cold. Another leader raised the possibility that swallowing light bulbs could disinfect. Any way you cut it, 31.1 million in Butler's tribe lack access to healthcare though its universal in some countries," said Gregor.

"They all had access to vaccinations, masks and testing," said Eminence.

"Many refused, insisting such precautions invited the government to infringe on their personal freedom," said Gregor.

"Dying doesn't restrict their freedom?" said Eminence. "They accept seat belts. And aren't they the same folks who let government tell a woman she can't have an abortion?"

"Logic is often a casualty in human decision making," said Gregor. "I've showed you countless examples - and how they deal with the termination of a human pregnancy is one of them. First, they can't agree on when life begins. Some insist it's at inception, some say, no, it's when a fetus is viable. Others say it's at birth. They fight over it, of course. Many want each homo sapiens female to decide if her pregnancy should continue, and there are rational reasons why a mother may not want her pregnancy. There's ectopic pregnancy - about 1 in 50 or 2%. Fetal malformation. There are social-criminal issues like incest or rape. But others insist that life must be protected from conception without exception – even when a medical issue threatens the mother's life. With two lives at stake, the mother's is expendable."

"So what do they do?" said Eminence.

"The ones most vehemently opposed to termination say they must protect life at any cost, so they bomb abortion clinics. They've killed physicians so they can't harm another fetus," said Gregor.

"They kill to honor life?" said Eminence.

"Doesn't happen. Well, not often," said Darius.

"Tell that to Barnett Slepian the Buffalo doctor shot down by a sniper," said Gregor. "And let me remind Eminence that those who oppose terminating a fetus want to limit how long they support life."

"Meaning what?" said Eminence.

"That they cherish babies from inception to delivery, just not afterwards. Life isn't so sacred once the child arrives. said Gregor.

"What nonsense are you spreading now?" said Darius.

"They fight, even kill, to protect a fetus. But once the child is born, whether it's fed, gets medical care, receives an education, has parents to raise it - that matters less to them. They have terms for care given following birth. They call it 'welfare', or the 'social safety net'. Many would do away with it," said Gregor.

"You exaggerate, Gregor," said Darius.

"Do I? Take healthcare. Many in Butler's tribe lobbied for years to secure medical care for every tribal member. They passed a healthcare act that added 11.3 million citizens to the roll of those covered. Opponents responded by voting seventy times to try take it away from them."

"I see why they rank 48th," said Eminence.

"I'll grant that occasionally humans are selfish," said Darius. "But many make incredible sacrifices so others are cared for – and at tremendous personal risk."

"Let me guess. A boy scout helps an old lady cross a busy street," said Gregor.

"No. Of the 17,107 kidney donors in a recent year, 5,537 came from living donors who risked surgical complications to give a kidney to another person - often saving the life of a total stranger. 169 million people in Butler's tribe are registered as possible donors. And you dare say humans can't be self-sacrificing," said Darius with a flurry of energy.

"A compelling example, Darius," said Eminence, "but I think we stray from the issue. The survival of the species itself is at stake. We should focus on that.

"Which brings us to Butler and Noah," said Eminence. "His plan for interplanetary emigration could save his species. Over the objections of Speaker Thermadore, the president has funded Project Noah and a launch date is set to expatriate the first passengers. An advance outpost has been robotically constructed on Mars which already grows vegetables, produces synthetic meat, and makes oxygen. It awaits human arrival."

"Then Parliament must decide the fate of homo sapiens once and for all," said Gregor. "It's not in the best interest of the Galaxy to allow them to launch. The species isn't salvageable. Let humans colonize Mars and who knows where they'll end up? Do we really want humans spreading through the galaxy like a pandemic?"

"Fair question," said Eminence. "It is time for Parliament to decide, and I'll call an Assembly."

"I'd like to speak for Butler and his species," said Darius.

"Good luck making that argument," said Gregor.

"You will be their spokesman, Provost Darius. But be mindful of the one-sentence rule," said Eminence.

"Pretty hard to sum up all human virtues in a sentence," said Darius.

"I can tell you what's wrong with them in two words," said Gregor. "They're irrelevant."

29

POWER OF THE PURSE

"**D**AMMIT CLAYMORE, IT's days to launch and we're nowhere," said Speaker Avril Thermadore.

"If you'd handled Billingsworth we wouldn't be here with our thumbs up our ass," said Majority Leader Senator Erling Claymore.

"Fuck you, Claymore. You agreed at every step."

"Whatever. But I'm afraid Butler's getting his launch," said Leader Claymore, "which leaves you and I screwed in the midterms."

"Hold your horses, Claymore," said Thermadore. "I have a thought."

"Any chance it's better than your last one," said Claymore.

Thermadore restrained his hand from grabbing Claymore's throat, then continued. "I directed the Office of General Council to petition SCOTUS to block spending for a launch that Congress never authorized."

"What makes you think they'll hear our case? They take only one hundred fifty of the seven thousand petitions they get, and even if they do, it'll be too late," said Leader Claymore.

"Chief Justice Sweindoffer will make it happen. We go way back to when I got Gammon to nominate him. He's lined up the four justices he needs so the case gets accepted and a writ of certiorari has been granted. We're on the docket," said Thermadore.

"It doesn't have to work it's way up the courts?"

"Sweindoffer explained that the court has original as well as appellate jurisdiction, allowing us to skip the trip up the lower courts. Our hearing is set for Tuesday, May 23. Sweindoffer when the court's six originalists will confirm the Executive lacks funding authority for Noah. The six justices would follow the constitution to hell and back to take the text literally and never have to interpret it. I'm confident they'll issue a stay.

That'll hold up NASA indefinitely or at least long enough to shut Noah down and kick Butler out on his black ass for wasting the money," said Thermadore.

"Excellent Thermadore, but are you one hundred percent sure they'll rule in time? They're weeks away from trucking StarShip to the launch pad."

"Sweindoffer says it will happen," said Thermadore.

■■■

Tuesday at 9 A.M. the Solicitor General and his legal team climbed the steps at the Court's west side entrance and walked past the seated marble figures – on the left the Contemplation of Justice, to her right, the male Guardian or Authority of Law, works of sculptor James Earl Fraser. They moved by the sixteen marble columns and through the massive, thirteen-ton bronze entrance doors.

The wood-paneled chamber remained much as completed in 1935, as the Marshal of the Court rose to announce the justices. At the sound of the gavel, all present stood while the robed justices entered and seated themselves at their regular places on the raised, wing-shaped, mahogany bench. Chief Justice Sweindoffer took his chair in the center, and from his far right, the Marshal of the Court uttered the traditional cry.

> "Oyez! Oyez! Oyez! All persons having business before the Honorable, the Supreme Court of the United States, are admonished to draw near and give their attention, for the Court is now sitting. God save the United States and this Honorable Court!"

The hearing began with lawyers for the plaintiff arguing that the Executive Branch lacked authority to fund a massive project like Noah; that congressional approval was mandatory and lacking. They argued that to allow the Executive to proceed would irreparably disrupt the balance of power between the legislative and executive branches. A point was made, not a matter of law but deemed worth making, that the nation's debt couldn't tolerate the $40 trillion burden the Executive branch would commit to.

Reminding yet again that the Noah budget was $20 trillion, lawyers for the Executive argued that without question the White House had authority to respond to emergencies; that it would be an abdication of responsibility should they fail to, and that now might be a good time for action with the loss of the human race pending.

At the end of the trial the justices held conference and votes were cast in order of seniority. The apolitical body split six to three - in this case with the originalists favoring the plaintiff, Speaker Avril Thermadore.

Assigned then written, the majority opinion noted that while the court was aware of Earth's impending doom, the justices felt duty bound to follow the law to the letter in accord with the constitution's perceived intent. Justice Pickenworth wrote the minority dissent noting that while the text of the law might lean against the Executive, to ignore common sense might be imprudent with the waters now covering the chamber's red carpet.

∎∎∎

The court having decided, back in the Speaker's office Avril Thermadore high-fived Senator Erling Claymore, his co-litigant.

"We finally got the bastard, Claymore," he said. Thermadore poured Crown Royal liberally into Baccarat glasses and they toasted.

"Noah's finished," said Claymore, "now get his Cabinet going on the 25th and we'll have the farmer out."

30

FLAME OUT

CHIEF OF STAFF Miley entered the Oval slowly, his face looking blanched. "Jesus, Mr. President, six to three. The court shut us down."

The President was slumped in his chair. "I don't know, Miley. I'd hoped the court might think it wiser for humanity to survive then to fine point the law to the depths of hell. Damn they make me mad."

"It's who they are," said Miley, "stuck in legal orthodoxy. They act like nothing's changed since 1789 when the Confederation Congress proclaimed the Constitution official. Their allegiance to strict interpretation stays pure, common sense be damned. But what do we do now, and what about you, Sir?"

Butler shrugged. "I don't know, Miley. We're out of options. Without funds, Project Noah is shut down, and we're about out of time. I'm thinking of returning to my farm, or what's left of it. I don't see much sense sitting around here like a eunuch at an orgy, waiting for Thermadore to impeach me again. All our work, wasted: the bills, our StarShip, the legal battles and for what? It won't be long before Thermadore, Madrid, and Claymore are sprawled out in this office plotting ways to strangle the voters … even as more cities flood. Does it matter where you and I go?"

"I'm so sorry, Sir," said Miley.

The President paused in thought, then spoke. "Miley."

"Sir?"

"Ask the Archivist to get me a copy of Nixon's resignation letter. I haven't a clue what I'd say," said the President. "Or who it goes to."

Miley was about to argue with the President, but decided this wasn't the time, "Right away, Sir."

The Archivist delivered a copy of Nixon's August 9, 1974 letter, addressed to Secretary of State Henry A. Kissinger. The President was surprised to find the letter was one sentence - a simple statement that Nixon hereby resigned the Office of the President.

"Miley, I don't see much point in continuing, but I want General Hooker's take on resignation. Is it the right thing to do for the people? Am I deserting them - millions of well-meaning, innocent folks who have done nothing to deserve what's coming?" said the President.

"I know. I know. This is new territory. Nixon's resignation is the only precedent I can think of, and if I may ironically paraphrase Senator Lloyd Bentsen, 'Mr. President, you're no Richard Nixon'," said Miley.

"At least I have that," said the President, looking past Miley.

"But the people, Miley," Butler shook his head.

"Do you suppose it would be any different if they took elections seriously, Sir? If they paid attention to the likes of Avril Thermadore? The penalty for not having done so is so great. Talk about reaping what you sow."

"I don't know what's right, Miley," said the President.

"Do you need some time, Sir?"

"Please, Miley."

The sun highlighted particles that slanted though the three south-facing windows behind the Resolute desk. The President looked up a moment, then sank to his knees, dropped his head and closed his eyes.

"Lord, my God. You sent me here to save them, and I have failed you. I am lost, defeated, I surrender. Thermadore and his kind - surely they can't be your agents - have won the day. My fellow Americans and all of my species - families, children, parents - will suffer because I didn't come through for them. I cannot endure the havoc I've caused those innocent beings. Lord, I beg you, end my life and bring me home from this Earth to your side. Show me the way out."

31

RESURRECTION

MILEY RETURNED TO the Oval after giving the President time to compose. The Chief of Staff found him at his desk, still staring blankly at the carpet, and he didn't look up.

"Sir," Miley reminded the President he'd returned.

The President eyed him, said nothing, and remained slouched.

"Anything I can get you?" said Miley.

The President remained silent, and Miley respectfully left the Oval again.

Butler's thoughts ran in a loop.

The farm, the livestock, my workers. Generations worked the land which is lost now because Jeremiah Butler couldn't get the job done. And losing my farm is a drop in the bucket compared to what humanity has already lost.

Pictures from CNB's flood coverage tore through his mind.

Helpless parents watch their young swept away by the flood and die trying to save them. And the hunger, the look on faces. I've let them down more than any President before me.

Butler let his head drop.

"Mr. President," Miley stuck his head in the Oval again. Butler waived him out.

The President closed his eyes. Slowly his fist began to clench.

This is my failure, but it's also Avril Thermadore's and his gutless minions. How does he lie to his people and not care, let them down over and over and do it with a smile. I've half a mind to take Thermadore, lock him in a room, and give him the kind of thrashing I've seen at the woodshed. I've tried to live by "thou shalt not kill," but I can't get the vision of putting a bullet through him out of my head. I couldn't do it. It would be yet one more way to defile the democratic process - whatever is left of it. But Jesus I'd like to put my fist through his bloated cheeks - along with Madrid and Claymore and the rest of them.

Butler felt his blood warm and his eyes energize as his jaw set tight.

Without thought he leaped up and shook his head as if casting off a bad dream. His face brightened. His chest filled. "Miley," the President bellowed, "Charlie Miley!"

Miley hurried in and stood before his boss. "Mr. President?"

"I'm not taking this," Butler slammed the Resolute desk with his fist. "Fuck Avril Thermadore."

Miley's jaw fell. Did he hear Butler correctly? He'd told his staff that in all the time he served the President, he never heard Jeremiah Butler, a man of quiet faith, swear - even in the privacy of the Oval - or among Congressional leaders for whom 'fuck' was a common pronoun.

"Get Hooker. And Billingsworth. Immediately, Miley," said the Jeramiah Butler the 56th President of the United States.

"Yes, Sir," said Miley, startled by his Commander in Chief's altered demeanor.

"What are you waiting for, Miley!"

"Yes Sir!" said Miley, now similarly energized and smiling as he hurried out.

■■■

The four met in the Oval. Miley, struck by the President's newfound vigor, marveled, *This isn't the quiet Jeremiah Butler I know."*

The President, his voice thundering, paced before his team, and then stopped. "Go with the launch, Gentleman."

"Sir?" said Miley.

"You heard me."

Hooker and Billingsworth looked at each other.

"But the court...?" said Miley.

"Get StarShip launched, Miley. I don't give a damn about the court."

"But...," said Billingsworth, wiping his forehead.

"Billingsworth, you make it happen and I mean soon. Hooker, as your Commander in Chief, I'm ordering you to surround StarShip with all the men you need - nothing less than a battalion. I want the StarShip protected until it's off. And Miley, get the Attorney General working on why this is legal."

"Have you considered...," said Hooker.

"...I have and I want it done, General. And be ready Hooker because you know Thermadore will come, and it won't be pretty. Get moving and we can beat him to the punch."

"Mr. President, are you sure?" said General Hooker. "You've considered the consequences if you defy the court. It'll be the end of your Presidency. I understand the greater imperative here, and I'm with you."

"...How fast can you get the ship off, Billingsworth," interrupted the President.

"Well...I...well," Billingsworth muttered, sweat dampening his bald scalp.

"And your Cabinet will invoke the 25th, Mr. President," said Hooker.

"He'll go to the press, petition the courts, hold hearings," said Miley. "It'll be epic."

"Let Thermadore bring it on. We'll be launched by then. Right, Billingsworth? How fast?"

"Well...I...well," Billingsworth repeated, eyes looking like you could pass right through them.

"Your Cabinet won't stick by you," said Miley. "As the General says, they'll invoke the 25th. Thermadore will get another impeachment, and this time they'll find you guilty."

"You'll see jail time, all of us will. But I fear what you'll face personally," said General Hooker.

"It's not about me, never has been, Hooker. What can they do after it's on its way? You can't call it back," said the President. "Get StarShip launched.

"Thermadore and the press will attack whatever we do. You know that. If it's not for the budget, it'll be for our failure to stop the floods. Or for the money we already spent on a StarShip that didn't launch. Let them impeach me, jail me... if they can before the floods come. There's nothing to loose. Get to it, gentlemen. A launch gives humans a chance."

32

THE CHAMBER OF DECISION

"FELLOW SELONS," EMINENCE began, "on the agenda is the matter of homo sapiens, Earth's dominant inhabitants. Having bungled management of their planet, normally we would leave them to their own destruction. But, while we are loath to override the Prime Directive and intervene, there is the matter of the planet's Xonium.

"We've asked if any conditions could make it possible for humans to govern effectively. For example, we tested to see if new leadership, driven by compassion and not beholden to donors, could create a government that serves all tribal members and administers to the needs of their planet.

"If it is your judgment that the species is not inherently flawed and that in time a rational government is conceivable, then homo sapiens will be allowed to survive. A nay vote results in termination. The matter will be decided now, before humans are allowed to launch and colonize beyond Earth.

"To present the case for quickly eliminating them, we have the highly respected, experienced guidance of Commander Gregor.

Commander Gregor beamed with pride.

"Arguing that humanity has enough merit to be preserved, we have the ever empathetic, much beloved Provost Darius.

Provost Darius glowed softly.

"Both leaders have for some time been helping Selon teams examine human nature, though their conclusions differ. Both have aided the Overseers in a test of humans, as we delve ever deeper and peel layers like an Earth onion, to try to answer the question of who they really are.

"Before they present their positions, and since Selons never weigh truth by word count, I remind Parliament and our opposing advocates that the One Sentence Rule applies in all decisions related to species. Selons value simple wisdom, effectively condensed.

"Each of you," Eminence sent vibrations to command the attention of both Darius and Gregor – "will give a one sentence argument and Parliament will deliberate in total silence. You have shared differing points of view, but now, since Selons find no value in *ad nauseam* repetition in the manner of a human trial, you each have one sentence to make your case. We are wise enough to glean meaning from brevity. Any questions?"

The chamber was silent.

In that case, I call upon Commander Gregor who presents in favor of elimination.

A circle of light appeared and brightened around Commander Gregor. "Fellow Selons, having eliminated diverse varieties of species unworthy of survival, I say from eons of experience that none behaved more illogically or with greater disregard for the survival of tribe and planet than the homo sapiens - who bring dysfunctionality to heights we cannot tolerate."

"Thank you, Commander Gregor. As always, your words carry powerful weight in this chamber," said Eminence.

"And now in favor of sustaining human life, our Provost Darius."

Darius too began to glow. "As I observe the homo sapiens, I find beauty in their emotionality, in their concern for others and in their drive for a better future - provided the best of them have a chance to lead, evolve and flourish."

"Thank you, Provost Darius" said Eminence. "How could we not admire the compassion that continues to enhance your reputation.

"Fellow Selons, before we vote, take what time you need to deliberate over Commander Gregor's and Provost Darius' points of view. Do we save or eliminate mankind?"

FOUR YEARS LATER

33

"He Laughs Best ..."

CONSTRUCTION FOR COLONIZATION had begun on Mars years before StarShip-1 hurriedly launched.

To get ready for first arrivals, robots extracted water from rich deposits of ice built up over thousands of years in the north polar region's icecap. It was stored along with fuel and oxygen in sufficient supply for the first StarShip passengers. Methane fuel was harvested and held for surface exploration and equipment relocation. Prior to man's arrival, an oxygen plant was completed and operational.

An ever-expanding array of solar panels provided power, despite their comparatively poor performance on Mars - only 43% of their efficiency on earth. To make up for their inefficiency, football-field-sized arrays of solar panels, printed on Mars, were placed to harvest the sun's energy.

Robots constructed rudimentary housing, standalone pods, using 3D printers loaded with Martian soil and sulfur to form cement. The material proved adequate to shield humans from the dangerous levels of radiation that penetrated Mars, since the planet lacked the magnetic fields that let Earth retain it's radiation-shielding atmosphere. Soon, multiple pods were joined to form a tiny colony.

Early colonists raised basic vegetables in a central greenhouse and every pod also had it's own vertical garden. Echoing Herbert Hoover, there was a chicken producing bioprinter in every kitchen replicating poultry and meat cells.

Colonists had difficulty adjusting to lower gravity, and in the beginning medical support was limited. But adjust they did, and the colony grew as more StarShips arrived carrying passengers and supplies; until the StarShips no longer come because terrible conditions on Earth made launching impossible.

To describe as 'difficult' what early Earth pioneers had to deal with would understate their determination. But, as Provost Darius routinely reminded his fellow Selons, man's survival was proof of the triumph of the human spirit.

The first children were born on Mars, and the human colony grew.

Mankind had saved itself, and many credited the determination of a modest Madison, Georgia born farmer, the 56th President of the United States, and more recently elected President of the United Mars Federation. By risking everything for colonization, he'd kept his species alive, and now led the new order of homo sapiens on Mars.

■■■

"Claymore, I have a plan," said Avril Thermadore.

"Not another one," said Erling Claymore.

"And National Survival Day festivities provide the ideal time to execute it," said Thermadore. "Butler and his staff are fully preoccupied with the hoopla celebrating our fourth year here."

"It's not only fun and games, Thermadore. Butler announced it's also a day to morn the billions he couldn't save," said Claymore. "I wouldn't call it hoopla."

"Celebrate. Mourn. Whatever. Some of us made it. Some got left. They saved my little woman, but between us, I'd as soon it had been my Chief of Staff. Jesus I miss those legs. Well, '*Que sera, sera*,'" said Thermadore.

"Since you're so fond of song titles Thermadore," said Claymore, "how about *Fools Rush In* since I'm dumb enough to ask what's up your sleeve now? The only plan you've succeeded with was getting Billingsworth to bump Madrid and Napalie so we got their seats on StarShip-2."

"I don't hear you bitching about that, Claymore," said Thermadore. "Feel free to thank me that we're not mourning you. But I know opportunity when I see it, and General Abizaid is key to what I'm thinking."

"General Abizaid? What can he do for us?" said Claymore.

"Tell me Claymore, what was the most important resource back home? What got folks into the one-percent?" said Thermadore.

"I don't know, diamonds?" said Claymore. "Food?"

"Nope, and up here there's too many mini-farms to control them all. Every pod has its garden," said Thermadore.

"Medicine?" said Claymore.

"Yes, for cancer radiation especially. But think even more basic," said Thermadore.

"Do we have to play this game Thermadore? Just spit it out for Christ's sake," said Claymore.

"Back home it was oil, wasn't it?" said Thermadore.

"Yes, but nobody's drilling for oil up here in case you hadn't noticed. So what's so valuable?" said Claymore.

"Oxygen, Claymore. Oxygen. It's produced and supplied in a single plant up here – at least until the second one goes on line and that won't be for a year. Here oxygen is way more critical than oil ever was back home. Control the oxygen plant, we rule Mars."

"Interesting, Thermadore. Basic, but it has merit. But you forget that General Abizaid's men guard the plant 24-7, and he doesn't think much of you," said Claymore. "His men have the only weapons on Mars, and he reports directly to Butler. He'd never buck his Commander in Chief. I'll grant you that if we could control the plant, we could dominate Mars. You could be President, Royalty... even God if you want to be worshiped. But it's not going to happen," said Claymore.

"'The Thermadore Dynasty' has appeal," said Thermadore.

"No doubt you think so," said Claymore, "but this is going nowhere."

"Someone else thinks it's a good idea," said Thermadore.

"Yeah? That wasn't smart," said Claymore. "You're the one who likes things close to the vest. You never told anyone but me when you thought about using sarin. So, who else did you tell?"

"General Abizaid," said Thermadore.

"Are you nuts," said Claymore. "He'd go straight to Butler."

"He didn't and he's with me one hundred percent," said Thermadore.

"I don't believe you. Butler gave him his stars," said Claymore.

"You're not up to date, my friend. Abizaid is sick of taking orders from Butler. Hates the President," said Thermadore, "and he's been confiding in me for some time."

"That's news if it's true. Control the oxygen plant. It could be very interesting," said Claymore. "But I don't believe Abizaid's with you."

"He is and the plant will soon be ours," said Thermadore.

Claymore stroked his chin patch. "Then hear me loud and clear, Thermadore. If what you say about Abizaid is true, know that before I'll go along with another of your cockamamie ideas and kiss your fucking ring again, you'll have to announce to everyone that I'm second in command. And I mean beforehand. I'd expect to hear it the minute we took control of the plant. I want it blasted on Mars-TV-1. Don't expect me to fall for the shit you pulled last time. You want my support, my title goes public ... Vice President Claymore, or Chancellor, Junior Monarch or whatever the fuck you have in mind," said Claymore.

"Claymore, Claymore. I only did that back home because it didn't matter. We had seats on the StarShip and you and I were leaving. That's the only reason I left you hanging at that press conference."

"It's non-negotiable. I'm not playing your game again, Thermadore."

"Consider it done, Claymore. The minute we have control there'll be a public announcement. We're meeting with Abizaid at the plant tonight to finalize the takeover."

"Tonight then," said Claymore.

"But come over here Claymore," said Thermadore.

"What?"

"Look out the porthole," said Thermadore.

"Okay, so?" said Claymore, looking at the vast emptiness of the dusty Martian surface.

"All that will be ours, Claymore."

■■■

Before leaving for his meeting that night, Avril Thermadore had the strangest sensation - the eerie feeling as if someone had entered his mind and was listening. It was an absurd thought, and he knew it, for no such surveillance equipment existed.

CHARACTERS

□ **Aadhilaz Jai** - Director of the President's National Economic Council and NASA authority. Annoys President Butler with a poor sense of humor

□ **Billingsworth** – head NASA Administrator

□ **Charlie Miley** – Chief of Staff to the President of the United States

□ **Chief Justice Sweindoffer** – head of SCOTUS

□ **Commander Gregor** – Selon charged with eradicating useless species

□ **Congessman Comenius Biggs** – Chairman of the House Oversight Reform Committee

□ **Congressman Gillmoe Jillings** – of West Virginia, up for reelection and overly fond of Wild Turkey

□ **Dr. Abraham Cotterswicken** – directs NASA StarShip deployment

□ **General Abizazid**– in charge of security on the Mars colony

□ **General Abraham Trufow** – Marine General

□ **Gorian Greggorhorn** – NASA's Noah Director of Cargo

□ **General Hooker** – Chairman of the Joint Chiefs of Staff

□ **Hickory Jamal** – Secretary of the Department of Agriculture

□ **Ken Brownstein** – Principal of Brownstein & Sheraton, D.C.'s largest lobbying firm

□ **Jeremiah Jeremy Butler** – black Georgia Farmer who becomes the 56th President of the U.S. when the lottery draws his name

□ **Majority Leader Senator Erling Claymore** – heads the U.S. Senate and an enemy of President Butler

□ **President Bernard Gammon** – 55th President of the US who dies of the plague

□ **Professor Saji** – NASA scientist who oversees much of Project Noah

□ **Provost Darius** – kindly Selon who champions the human cause

□ **Seer** – Selon magistrate who provides reports on the galaxy species

☐ **Senator Creedence Rawlings** – sponsor of bills HR-1,HR-2 and HR-11 and a Butler supporter

☐ **Senator Rubin Hallingsworth** – Kentucky climate change denier who insists the Selons don't exist - until he's dissolved

☐ **Senator Julius Napalie** of Missouri – opposes President Butler and intends to thwart his agenda

☐ **Senator Tobias Madrid** – ally of Avril Thermadore who plots against President Butler with Thermadore.

☐ **Speaker of the House Avril Thermadore** – leader of the House of Representatives and third in line for presidential succession

☐ **Vice President Eleanor Winslow** – 2nd in line for succession who assumes she'll be president after President Gammon dies in office

OTHER BOOKS BY I. MICHAEL GROSSMAN

Non-Fiction

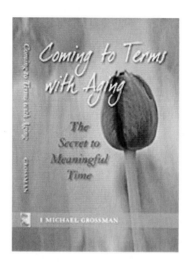

Coming to Terms with Aging: the Secret to Meaningful Time, RDR books

Memoir

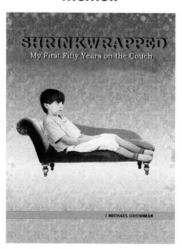

Shrinkwrapped: my first fifty years on the couch, RDR Books

Adult Children's Adventure

Mike the Moose: Master of Marbles, EBook Bakery

Ethical Fantasy/Adventure

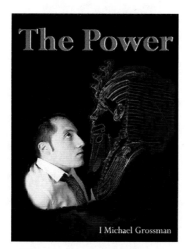

The Power, EBook Bakery

Fiction

The Realm - the Fable of Morality - EBook Bakery

Poetry

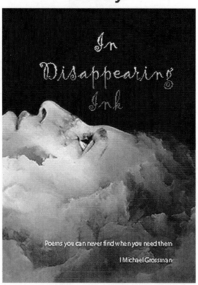

In Disappearing Ink: poems you can never find when you need them -
EBook Bakery

About the Author

The Accidental President is I. Michael Grossman's seventh book. Grossman's six other books run the gamut from poetry to an adult children's book and from fiction to non-fiction.

Articles span similarly diverse topics for *Advertising Age, Ergo Solutions* magazine, *The CLIA Cruise Industry Annual Report, The American Banker,* and *Plane & Pilot* magazine.

Grossman holds a B.A. and M.A. from Michigan State University. He taught English and Journalism at Oakland Community College before leaving academia for what he was told would be *"the real world."* He created *The Science of Your Own Success*, a course taught at the New School in Manhattan, then started four businesses including Cruises of Distinction and Office Organix.

"I sold my last two ventures because I had a book to write," says Grossman, referring to his memoir, *Shrinkwrapped: my first fifty years on the couch.*

Grossman currently runs EBookBakery.com and helps fellow authors self-publish. His own books have been both traditionally published and self-published.

The 'I.' is the author's full first name and not an abbreviation. "I claim no responsibility for the name though I participated in the birth," quipped Grossman. Michael, his therapist wife Susan and a varying number of four-legged creatures share blessed lives in Rhode Island.

Please help by offering your review at Amazon.com
Go to the book, scroll down, click on 'Review This Product'.
Thank you!

26358436R00093